THE CROSSING

2

-BETRAYAL-

Alice Hepworth

BC
BAD CREATIV3

BAD CREATIVE BOOKS

This book is a work of fiction. Names, characters, places and incidents are products of the author's imagination or are used fictitiously. Any resemblance to actual events or locales or persons, living or dead, is entirely coincidental.

ISBN 9798685156327

Cover art by Gestvlt

Cover artwork copyright © 2020 by BadCreative

OTHER BADCREATIVE BOOKS

Banking On Love
The Jaguar King
Bewitching Amelia
The Crossing
Managing Complications In Anesthesia And Critical Care

Table Of Contents

<u>Chapter 1</u>

Berkeley. 8 years ago. 11:20 p.m.

A young man sat staring outside the window of a large house. He stared at the passing cars and the brightly lit shop windows with such deep contemplation. There was seemingly a lot on his mind, and after a few minutes or so, he let out a deep breath and got up from where he sat. He had reached a decision as he opened his closet and took out a varsity jacket. 'The night was going to be cold after all', he thought as he zipped up the jacket, took a bag and walked out of his room and down the hall.

He was stopped in his tracks for a moment when another man called out to him from his room. "Hey man, where you headed?"

"Just going out for a walk." He quickly replied. "Might grab some six packs and stuff along the way."

"Think you can get me some Red Bull?" He asked.

The young man nodded and was soon on his way. He let out a sigh of relief as he walked down the stairs and out of the large house. He pulled out his keys and got into his Jeep. He started the Jeep and drove into the streets. There was a destination he was heading out to and he had to get there before midnight. It was only 20 minutes away, but with the sudden reroute, he feared he would get there in no less than 30 minutes.

He couldn't let that get to him. So he quickly took a detour and drove down the alternate route. He made several turns around blocks and streets until he was out of the city and into what looked like an abandoned road. "Gotta get there before midnight." He kept muttering to himself as he checked his digital watch every now and then. He saw that it was 11:50!

'Come on', he told himself. 'Let me get there before midnight'. At last, he reached his destination. He took out a pocket flashlight, got out of the car and walked towards a road that fanned out in a perfect cross. There were several piles of stones and gravel in each direction, and at the center of the crossroad was a gnarled tree with several dark and decaying branches sticking out like bony fingers.

"This must be it." He thought, shining his pocket flashlight on the tree's trunk. He checked his watch. It was 11:58. Two minutes till midnight. He had made it just in time. He looked around, checking each direction for anyone or thing coming his way. "She should be here." He said out loud, the cold breath escaping from his lips as he zipped up his jacket even further. "No, maybe I should wait a little longer." He heard the first beep of midnight from his digital watch.

'Wait for the 12th bell.' He reminded himself. 'She's bound to show up.' As the 12th bell rang out, the young man almost felt like this was a waste of his time until he heard a gentle neigh in the distance, followed by the trotting sound of hooves and the alluring sound of twinkling bells.

He looked up to see a large white horse with a smooth, white velvet pelt, and beautiful trusses of white and blonde hair standing before him. Sitting astride the horse on a beautiful jewel encrusted saddle, was an elegant looking woman dressed entirely in white silk, with gold trimmings on her clothes and layers of silk and satin draped around her. Her face was partially covered with a silk veil that had rows of small gold coins at the brim. She had numerous rings on her fingers in every shape and style. Each ring would have a small jewel surrounded by smaller diamonds. On her feet were golden sandals and anklets with multiple gold bells attached on them.

The young man looked at the beautiful woman. She then spoke in a soft and otherworldly voice. "What do you ask of me?" The young man took a deep breath and replied.

"To leave a legacy unlike no other…"

The woman reached for one of the rings on her fingers, pulled it off and gave it to the young man before riding away into the darkness.

****

The only time you would see a crime scene is usually on those crime dramas or live news coverage. Usually, you would see police officers interrogating witnesses and victims alike, while the crime scene and medic teams would be taking care of both injured and deceased bodies. What makes it different is that you are watching it from the comfort of your own home. It's a lot different if you were actually there. Even more so when you're being interrogated by the police.

That was what was going through Jonathan Madden's mind as he and Artemis Rosi sat by an open ambulance while a team of paramedics checked their vitals. After all, seeing someone getting run over by a truck would have certain medical side effects that could be permanent. Post-traumatic stress disorders, anxiety and increased blood pressure, just to name a few. A medic did one last check on Jonathan. "Hmm, looks normal to me." He said. "Your blood pressure's alright."

Another medic, who was attending to Artemis, added. "I know you're a bit tense. I need you to squeeze on this. It will help release the tension." He handed her a small rubber ball. Meanwhile, three paramedics were wheeling in a gurney that had a closed body bag lying on top of it. A police officer approached the two teenagers and said. "Can you identify the body for us please?"

"I'm sorry, what?" Jonathan asked as the gurney approached them. "You want us to identify Claire again?"

"For legalities sake, I'm afraid." He replied. "After that, I have some questions for the both of you." He gestured to one of the paramedics to unzip the body bag. Artemis quickly covered her mouth and felt right into the corners. Jonathan looked away for a brief moment before focusing his gaze back at it. The mangled and bloody face that was once the beautiful Claire O' Hara emerged in between the plastic folds.

"That is Claire O' Hara." Artemis said, still covering her mouth. "She's a student at Berkeley." The paramedic then zipped up the body bag once more before wheeling the gurney away. "I feel sick." Artemis whispered to Jonathan. And who could blame her? He thought. After all, we just witnessed a person getting run over by a speeding truck. Who wouldn't feel sick at the thought of it?

"Alright, you two." The police officer said as he took out a notepad and pen. "I have a security guard who tells me she spoke to the both of you before her filming. And several witnesses say that right after she went berserk and ran off, you two followed her."

"What of it?" Jonathan asked. "Are you saying we had something to do with-"

"Oh not at all." The officer said. "I would just like to know how you know her and what your conversation was about."

"Well, she's my roommate." Artemis said. "But apart from that, not much other than she suddenly started getting lucky at things."

"Is it presumptuous of me to say that both you and the victim were not on good terms?" The officer asked scribbling in his notepad.

"I wouldn't say that..." she replied. "We are not close, but that doesn't mean I don't like her. We wanted to warn her about-"She stopped midsentence as Jonathan gently squeezed her hand. She understood why he did that; if they were to tell the entire truth, the officer would think they were crazy.

"About hubris." Jonathan said, finishing Artemis' statement. "We wanted to warn her that all that fame could get into her head."

"I see..." The officer said, writing more notes. "And you felt the need to go after her when she ran?"

"We were worried she could hurt herself or others." She added. Jonathan could tell that the police officer was giving them the suspicious look. He let out a silent sigh as the officer kept his notepad.

"Well, if you have any more information, do let us know." He said as he walked away to the ambulance.

"Do you want me to take you home?" Jonathan asked. Artemis nodded as Jonathan gently helped her up. The two of them walked towards Jonathan's scooter, and as they put on the helmets, Artemis said. "We did see what we saw, right? We weren't imagining it, right?"

She was referring to the ghastly sight of the Lady on the Horse. A chill ran up Jonathan's spine just thinking about it. He had never before seen a terrifying sight that would make him question the very nature of what is real and what is imaginary. He could simply say that it was an image caused by heightened stress levels and the need for logic. But he saw it plain as day, and what made it more terrifying was that Artemis saw it too. "We didn't imagine it, right?"

"Want to get something to eat?" Jonathan asked as he started the scooter. "There's this great, all night diner that serves the best stuffed peppers and burgers."

He heard a grumbling sound coming from both their stomachs. 'Yeah,' he thought. 'Some food sounds good right about now.' Artemis got on the scooter and both of them sped off towards the all-night diner. While they were going through the streets, Jonathan couldn't help but feel uneasy. He had always been a rational young man who often found logic and reasoning behind things. And this was one instance where reasoning couldn't be explained.

They arrived at an all-night diner called Sam's Place. It was, as best as one could describe, the quintessential All-American diner. It had red leather upholstered seats and brown Formica topped tables. The walls were plastered with framed posters and pictures of iconic and vintage Americana images. They found a booth seat by a window and sat there while a waitress walked over and handed them the menus. "Welcome to Sam's Place, home of the best pies and burgers in the city." She said with a warm smile. "What can I get for you, dears?" She noticed the slightly pale look in Artemis and Jonathan's face. "Oh my, are you both alright?"

"Yeah, we're fine." Jonathan replied looking at the menu. "Umm, we'll have the tomato soup, the double cheese and beef burger and fries and maybe some of Granny Sam's apple pie."

"Want any coffee with that?" she asked.

"Maybe some cold soda." He replied. The waitress nodded and took the menus and walked back to the kitchen. Jonathan looked at Artemis, who was still visibly shaken. "Hey, come on." He said holding her hand. "Just take a deep breath and when dinner comes, we'll eat."

"How could you think of food at a time like this?" Artemis said, slowly raising her eyebrows. "We saw Claire get run over by a truck and then we saw something that I can't even explain."

"We're not in the right state right now." He said just as the waitress returned with their orders. "So we should just get our knives and forks and eat." He took the plate of burger and fries and began to eat it with gusto.

"Seriously?" She said as she took some soup. "Tell me again why we're eating dinner after witnessing something freaky?"

"Food helps me think and calm down." He replied. "When there is something that I can't comprehend on the spot, I usually eat something like a Twinkie or a Big Mac."

"Wow, who would have thought you would stress eat?" Artemis said.

"Believe it or not, it was my older brother Alex who taught me this." He said, drinking his cold soda. "There was a time when Alex was so swamped with his studies that he asked me to go with him, and we both snuck out and got in his Jeep to eat at Taco Bell. We ate a lot of Tacos and Quesadillas that night." He laughed at the memory. "Ever since then, I usually eat something whenever I feel overwhelmed. It helps me see things a lot clearer."

"Wow." Artemis said as she finished her meal. "You know, now that I think about it. I do feel a bit better. I mean, given after what we had seen of course."

"I know." Jonathan said with a more somber note in his tone. "Believe me when I say this, I can't even comprehend it myself." He drank the ice-cold soda and added. "The Lady on the Horse...who is she?"

"I haven't found anything in my books on who the Lady is." Artemis said. "But there are similar stories about ladies who became iconic riding on horses."

"Maybe if we started on the origin of the rhyme and the ritual, we might find something." He said as he paid for the dinner and got up. "Come on, I gotta get you back to the dorm. I imagine there will be a lot of people who will ask what happened the moment we get back on campus." Something unavoidable unfortunately, he thought to himself. After all, most likely the news of a rising star's demise and the witnesses would be broadcasted on various media platforms.

It was something he wanted to avoid as much as possible. But there was no helping it. Artemis nodded, completely understanding the possible predicament they would eventually be subjected to. As they walked out of the diner and got on Jonathan's scooter, Artemis then asked.

"Do you think Claire's the only one who's done the ritual?"

"What do you mean?" Jonathan asked.

"I mean, "Artemis clipped the helmet on. "What if there were others who also asked the Lady for something?"

"That would be a long list." He replied. "But in any case, if we can find the source and a way to avert it, that's probably the best we can do." The scooter then sped off taking the two students back to Berkeley, hoping at the very least that most of the students were all tucked in bed.

****

After dropping Artemis in her dorm, Jonathan made his way back to his dorm. He parked the scooter in the usual parking slot at the back of the dorm. But while he was putting the padlock on, he stopped for a moment and felt all sorts of anger inside of him. He somehow felt that it was his fault. After all, the only reason Claire made a deal with the Lady on the horse was because he had refused to even acknowledge her. If he had just given her the time and day and perhaps the attention, she wouldn't have resorted to doing something like that.

'No', he told himself. 'You're not at fault, Jonathan.' She made her own decision. He let out a sigh and slowly walked inside the dorm. He climbed up the long staircase and entered his dorm room, only to be met by a rather shocked and upset Dick.

"Jonny! What the hell man!?" He exclaimed, dragging Jonathan inside and seizing him by the collar of his shirt. "What is this I hear about Claire being killed and you witnessing it?!"

"Wow news travels fast." Jonathan sarcastically said. "Mind letting go of my shirt, Dick? I'm not in the mood."

"You better tell me what the hell happened" He demanded, slowly letting go of Jonathan's shirt.

"It's just as you said." Jonathan pulled off his shirt and tossed it in the hamper. "Claire got into an accident with a truck and Artemis and I were there. I don't see why you're so upset about it."

"You're damn right I'm upset." Dick said. "I was going to ask her out and now I won't be able to."

"Like you had any chance with her." He muttered. "Look, it was a freak accident and we couldn't do anything at all." He put on a clean shirt and got into bed. "Listen, I'm tired and I don't want to deal with this right now. Okay?" He pulled the bedsheets over his body and tucked himself in. He did his best to ignore Dick's pandering and drifted off to sleep. Now wasn't the time to think about it. Not yet at the very least. After all, it wasn't easy to get over witnessing someone get killed in front of you. He closed his eyes, wondering just how Artemis was handling it.

****

There was a loud banging sound coming from the door the next morning. Jonathan groggily got up, walked to the door and opened it. "Yes?" he asked yawning a bit. "What do you-Milo?!" He exclaimed as Milo Garnier rushed inside the room and closed the door behind him.

"Ah mon-ami." He said "Mon dieu, you don't look so good."

"I just woke up." He yawned. "Anyway, what do you want?"

"Is it true? What zey're saying all over ze dorm?" Milo asked in a frenzy.

"What are you talking about?" Jonathan asked, clearly not in any good mood whatsoever.

"Is it true zat Claire O' Hara was killed in a truck accident and you were zere?" he finally finished. Jonathan groaned as he pulled out a shirt and pants. 'News does travel fast,' he thought to himself as he went to the bathroom. "Hey Milo, can you just give me like 20 minutes to wash up? You can sit there on my chair and wait." He called from the bathroom.

13

Milo sat on Jonathan's desk as he heard the shower run. He noticed the slightly messy bed next to an organized and fixed bed. "So, where's your roommate?"

"Out doing football tryouts. "He replied from the bathroom. "He usually sleeps in, but only gets up early for football tryouts."

"Ze typical meat head, no?" Milo said as soon as Jonathan walked out of the bathroom. "So tell me, is it true?"

Jonathan dried himself off and changed into a black shirt and blue jeans. He sat on the bed and began to towel dry and comb his hair. "Well, to be honest." He began. "I wasn't going to go out the night before. But Artemis called me and she sounded frantic."

"Oh la la la..." Milo grinned. "La belle fille' calls you? Zis is quite a love story, no? So what did she need?"

"She sounded frantic and asked me to take her to the filming location." He replied. "I asked her why and she-" He stopped for a bit. If he told Milo the reason for Artemis's frantic request, Milo would most likely think they were crazy. 'Tone it down a bit,' he told himself. He continued. "She was worried about her roommate, Claire."

"Mon dieu! The plot, she thickens no?" Milo said. "Did you know she was her roommate?"

"At first, no. But we met her once and honestly...I didn't like her."

"Oh why?"

Jonathan looked at Milo and replied. "She sort of...embarrassed Artemis."

"C'est horrible" Milo exclaimed. "Zat is not very nice at all. But why would Artemis be worried about her roommate who does not treat her with respect? Zat is a curious thing, indeed."

"I don't know." Jonathan and Milo then heard a ping sound coming from Jonathan's laptop. He opened his laptop and saw that it was an instant message from Artemis. Upon seeing Artemis' face on the user ID, Milo whistled and replied.

"Sacre' bleu! She is indeed la belle femme! Ah mon ami, you are a lucky man."

"She's just a friend, Milo." Jonathan said, trying his best to hide his flustered cheeks and opening the message to read it. He furrowed his eyebrows and read each line. "Oh my god."

"What is ze matter?" Milo asked.

"It seems Artemis woke up to her neighbors asking her about what happened last night." He sighed and picked up his bag and keys. "I'd better get her or else she'll be late."

"Ahh, ze gallant knight on his way to save le belle femme!" Milo said. Just then, the door swung wide open and Dick walked inside, dressed in a loose shirt over football shoulder pads, jogging pants and sneakers. He looked at Milo and then at Jonathan. "Oh, didn't know you had company, Jonny. You heading out?" He noticed Jonathan had already his backpack on.

"Yeah. I have to go somewhere." He replied.

"Take the fire escape if you want to avoid the crowd outside." Dick said. "Some of the guys want to know what went down last night."

'Great,' Jonathan thought. 'Just what I needed.' He thanked Dick for the advice and added. "Milo, I have to go so..."

"Say no more, mon ami." Milo replied. "La belle Artemis awaits you."

"He's going to see his girl?!" Dick exclaimed, suddenly getting up. "Sweet, I earned $300!"

Leave it to Dick to make anything involving Artemis a bet. Jonathan groaned as he slipped on his hoodie and opened the door just a bit to see the hallway. He didn't see anyone...yet. He took a deep breath, opened the door and crept out of his room. He walked briskly towards the fire escape and got out of the door. He hurried down the wrought iron stairs and landed on the ground. He drew his hood up and began to walk towards the girl's dormitory.

All he wanted was just to have a regular college experience like cramming for exams, probably watch some football games, get drunk whenever he could, meet interesting friends and possibly...a girlfriend. Just normal stuff. Not unwanted notoriety. He pulled out his phone and sent a message to Artemis, while doing his best to obscure his face with his hoodie. As he approached the girl's dormitory, he suddenly heard a trotting sound. A horse? He stopped in his tracks and looked around. He saw a student playing a set of bongos in a steady rhythm.

'Just drums,' he thought, letting out a sigh of relief. Upon reaching the girls' dormitory, he stood by a large tree, pulled out his phone and called Artemis.

"Hey...I'm here. I'm by the tree in front of your dorm." He said as he looked at the building. 'She can't go through the front door,' he thought as he leaned against the tree and waited for her to come out. 'Most likely she'll go through the fire exit.' He looked at building's tall windows and overhanging ledge. 'Or maybe she could go through the windows and walk across the ledge.' He thought. 'It's closer to the fire escape than going through the hallway.'

Suddenly, he jumped as he felt a hand touch his shoulder. He turned around to see Artemis, dressed in a jacket and hat with a scarf covering half of her face. "God, you scared me. What the hell?!" he exclaimed, letting out short breaths. "Wait, how did you get out of your dorm? I didn't see you..."

"I was out of the dorm before you came in." Artemis said, pulling the scarf down so that she could speak clearly. "I had to climb out through the window and walked across the ledge." 'I was right, somewhat.' Jonathan thought. He then noticed her exhausted looking face. "I take it you didn't have a good night's sleep as well?" He asked.

"Let's just get some breakfast out." She said as she wrapped the scarf back around her face. "Some place where they can't recognize us."

****

The smell of crisp, fried bacon mixed with omelettes, pancakes and potato hash browns made Jonathan and Artemis's mouths water with anticipation. They sat in a booth at the all-night diner they had gone to the night before, and began to eat their breakfast. A waitress walked over and poured them each a cup of freshly brewed coffee.

"Now that hits the spot." Jonathan said, thanking the waitress and taking a swig of the coffee. "Hmm, that tastes good. Can I get seconds on the pancakes?"

"No problem, dear." The waitress replied. "And seconds for your girlfriend, too?"

"Oh, I'm not his girlfriend." Artemis quickly said, turning red. The waitress looked at her and then at Jonathan before giving a little giggle and replying. "I'll be back with two more pancakes, dears." As she walked away, Jonathan cut into his pancakes and ate it along with his omelette and hash browns. He silently thought about what the waitress had said. Girlfriend? She thought Artemis was his girlfriend? He could feel his heart beat a little faster whenever he thought of that.

'She's just a friend, Jonathan.' He told himself. 'A friend who happens to like your company. A friend you seem to like very much. Had he ever considered the likelihood that maybe it would be nice to have her as one.' "Jonathan?" Artemis' voice broke his train of thoughts and he somehow focused his attention back to her.

"Yes?" he asked looking at her.

"You really are something." Artemis said as she sprinkled some maple syrup on the pancakes. "How is it that you're so calm?"

'Better not dwell on that idea yet.' He thought to himself. "Believe me, I'm not." He quickly replied. "But I have to be. Cause when I'm calm, I can think clearly." He bit into a hash brown and added. "So, you didn't have a good night's sleep huh?"

"The first thing I ran into when I got back were the girls cornering me at the hallway." Artemis groaned. "It's freaky how fast news spreads."

"Well, we live in an age where it is." He said. "And then, let me guess, they started asking you what were you doing there?"

She nodded and groaned. "I didn't say anything. I mean, do you think anyone will believe me if I said, 'Hey, I had this really bad feeling that Claire will be in trouble because I saw a creepy looking lady in the car with her.'?" She quivered at the thought.

"Even I myself wouldn't believe it if I didn't know the circumstances." Jonathan noticed a group of people in another booth looking at them every now and then while talking among themselves. This was just the kind of thing he wanted to avoid. But there was no helping it.

"I know that look." Artemis said as she looked over her shoulder and sighed. "So what do we do now? "

"We find out where this game started and see if there is a loophole of sorts." He said. "And I think I might know someone who does."

She looked at Jonathan and lowered her head while putting her hands on top of the table. "I had a really nasty nightmare about it last night."

"What was the nightmare about?" he asked. Artemis held both her hands as she tried to find the right words for it. She reached for her cup of coffee and drank it all in one gulp.

"I dreamt I was standing at a crossroad." She replied. "At least, I think it's me. There were large, trees that had no leaves and there was mist all over the place. I kept asking myself how I got there when I suddenly heard a clip clopping sound, and then I would see a strange shape coming towards me. It looks like a dark lady on a dark horse with red eyes. When it becomes clear, it's a skeleton dressed in a white robe on a skeleton horse."

She called for the waitress for a refill on the brewed coffee. Once the waitress finished pouring the coffee into her mug, Artemis continued. "I'm running, but I can't seem to know where I'm going. And she's right behind me. Before she can even reach me, I wake up."

"That is scary." Jonathan said.

"I know. I don't understand why I'm dreaming about it." Artemis drank her cup one more time. Jonathan scratched his chin thoughtfully. Then he asked. "Have you ever considered summoning her?"

PTOO! Artemis spat her coffee at the question. "Oh my God, no!" she exclaimed. "I mean, I did once. But if what happened to Claire would be the result, then I'd rather stay alive than end up...dead." She gulped at the last word. Jonathan let out a small chuckle and after a few seconds, Artemis too giggled.

The two of them decided to talk about other things. After all, it was early in the morning and they did go to the diner to forget about last night's affair. Even if it was for a brief moment. They then finished their breakfast, paid the bill and headed out of the diner. As they walked along the cobbled streets back to the university complex, Jonathan began to think. Where could the game have possibly started? Was it something like a bastardization of age-old fortune telling rituals and practices in many cultures around the world? He then thought about Artemis's nightmare. Why was she having that nightmare? Could it mean that Artemis could be tempted to try and call on the Lady on the Horse?

'No'. He thought. 'Artemis is a rational girl. She would never do something like that and endanger her own life.' He looked at Artemis, who smiled at him. He quickly hid his slightly red face. Maybe he really did care about her. After all, he did leave his dorm to get her. He did feel a lot happier being with her, Maybe....just maybe...

They made it back to campus where they saw a large crowd gathered around what looked like an ebony black SUV. It was parked in one of the parking lots outside the main building. They could see a lot of students had their phones out and were taking pictures of themselves with the car.

"Wow, looks like some celebrity is visiting." Artemis said. "Look at that car! Must be someone really famous." They made their way to the crowd and stared at the luxurious car. Jonathan, however, took one quick look at the car and the plate. He then knew who it belonged to. He let out a groan that only Artemis could hear.

"Why is he here ?!" He muttered.

<u>Chapter 2</u>

The University of California, Berkeley has been a celebrated institution for almost 150 years. It has produced many prominent and influential alumni over the years such as actors Gregory Peck, Ashley Judd and Stacy Keach, costume designer Edith Head and even famous athletes like Jonny Moseley and Aaron Rodgers. It is often said that if you are an alumni from Berkeley, it is a guarantee that you will be landed with a lucrative job.

At least, that what was often ingrained in every potential applicant when they consider applying to Berkeley. But every so often, it is hard to get into the illustrious school. Certain things had to be considered. There was the applicant's academic aptitude and whether or not they would commit to the grueling years of study and work. Then there is how involved they are in their school with extracurricular activities like the school paper, the debate club and even the school band. Then there is also the GPA's to take note of. Finally, although it is quite rare, there is the likelihood that one's standing be put into play.

For the most part, applicants are generally screened based on the aforementioned criteria. However, there is an unspoken criterion of sorts, where applicants whose relatives were alumni of the college would have a higher chance of being accepted. They would be known as legacies.

When Jonathan Madden filled up his college application, there was only one school he had set his heart on. Albeit it would be a stretch since he knew that getting into Berkeley would be hard. After all, he didn't have that much school involvement other than the literature club. And his grades, although they were acceptable, would not meet with the college's standards. Still, he was hopeful. And when he received his acceptance letter, he felt a sense of joy. But also, a bit of disappointment as well.

If there was one thing he wanted more than anything, it was to get into the college of his dreams on his own merit; he didn't like the idea that he would be accepted solely on the fact that his father and brother were Berkeley alumni. And when he found out that he was accepted after his brother interceded on his behalf, he had grown to loathe and resent the fact that he was the younger brother of a successful Berkeley alumnus.

"Jonathan, are you okay?" Artemis asked, noticing the slight scowl forming across his face.

"Why is he here?" Jonathan muttered through gritted teeth and clenched his hand into a fist. He made his way past the crowd and into the building, with Artemis following behind him. He walked up the stairs to the second floor and into a long hallway with rather long strides.

"Hey, wait up." Artemis called out, catching up to him. "Jonathan, what's wrong? What's got you so worked up all of a sudden?"

"I can't believe he showed up." He replied as he approached a large door at the left of the hallway. "Why is he even here?"

"Who's here?" she asked.

Jonathan sighed and replied. "You'll see." He opened the door of the room and walked in. Inside were two men having a conversation. One was a man in his mid-40s to early 50s dressed in a business casual suit. This man was Mr. Hart, a member of the Alumnae Association.

The other man was in his early 30s with sleek black hair and handsome hazel eyes. He was dressed in a smart casual attire. But it only took one look at his face for Artemis to slowly guess who this man was. But before she could register who he was, Jonathan scowled and said. "What the hell are you doing here, Alex?"

Alex? As in Alex Madden? His older brother? She thought to herself.

"Nice to see you too, little brother." His older brother, Alex said. There was a somewhat calm and distinguished tone in his voice and the way Alex carried himself, as though he were a polished gentleman. This was a complete contrast to Jonathan, who, although seemed proper and calm, displayed a rather rebellious façade.

"Mr. Madden, your behavior is appalling." Mr. Hart exclaimed, slightly scolding Jonathan. "Why would you speak to your brother like that?"

"Oh Mr. Hart, don't worry." Alex said. "This is how we greet each other. It's our term of endearment."

'What the hell, Alex?' Jonathan thought. 'What are you trying to pull?' Mr. Hart looked at Alex and then at Jonathan, before letting out a deep breath and continued. "I see. Well then, I hope to see you every now and then, Alex." He shook Alex's hand. "I think I should give you boys some time to catch up." He then turned on his heel and left the room.

Jonathan folded his arms and looked at his brother. "Well, Alex. Care to tell me what my older brother is doing here?"

"You know that attitude of yours is going to bite you in the back, right?" Alex said. Then he noticed Artemis standing behind

Jonathan. Smiling, he walked past his brother and asked. "And who is this beautiful lady?"

"She's my friend, Artemis. Artemis Rosi." Jonathan replied, feeling a bit slighted at how his brother simply walked past, as if he were dismissing Jonathan. Alex walked up to Artemis, took her by the hand and gave a curtly bow.

"'En chante', Mademoiselle." He greeted. "It's rare for my little brother to have a new friend with him. Especially a girl. You must be a very special friend of his."

"We're just friends." She replied, a hint of uneasy embarrassment slowly swelling in her tone. "So you're the famous Alex Madden." She looked at him from head to toe. She had to admit; he was quite good looking and just about anyone would fall for him. It was almost understandable why Claire O' Hara had an almost borderline obsession with wanting to date either Alex or Jonathan.

"You didn't answer my question, Alex." Jonathan said. "What are you doing here?"

"I was invited here." He replied. "How about we continue this talk elsewhere? Is the Underground Brew still around?"

"Yeah, but Artemis and I have classes." Jonathan said. "We can't just up and leave."

"That is true." Alex said. "If you're going to have a bright future ahead of you, you have to attend your classes. "

"Thanks for stating the obvious." Jonathan muttered sarcastically under his breath as Alex walked to the door. "Aren't you supposed to be signing some big contract upstate?"

"I was." He replied. "But then, like I said earlier, I got a call from the university and they wanted to see me right away."

"And you happily obliged." Jonathan said. Artemis could sense there was a rather irritated tone in his voice; it was like he was upset that his brother was here. 'There must be a reason,' she thought. Alex looked at Jonathan and sighed. "And I'm hearing something about you witnessing an accident?"

"Wow, how did that reach your ears?" He asked.

"Care to tell me what happened?" Alex asked.

Jonathan grunted and brushed him aside. "Come on Artemis, let's get going." He said as the two of them walked to the door and left. Alex then followed the two of them as they walked along the hallway, passing several awe-struck students. Jonathan could feel the gaze fixated entirely on them. Something he had desperately wanted to avoid ever since his first day. "I really hate this." He muttered.

"Hate what, little brother?" Alex asked. They reached the main door when Jonathan stopped abruptly. He looked at Alex with an annoyed and almost angry look.

"This!" He replied gesturing to how everyone was now staring at them. "Do you think I like people looking at us every time we walk together? Do you think it's a nice feeling being known as the little brother of an all-star alumni?"

"You can always ignore them." Alex said. "Like I have always said. You are defined only by what you do, not by others."

"Oh and I suppose you had nothing to do with my application getting approved." Jonathan said. "I really got into Berkeley on my own merit?"

"Well...." The tone in Alex's voice was more than enough for Jonathan to draw his own conclusion. He sighed and said. "Look, Artemis and I have class to go to. So I'll just see you when I can."

Grabbing Artemis by her hand. Jonathan and Artemis walked through the door, braving the large crowd that had gathered around the door, leaving Alex completely speechless.

****

To say that it was a rather eventful morning for Jonathan would be the understatement of the day. He tucked his hands in his pocket as he walked to his class. He tried his best to ignore the group of students talking among themselves as he walked past them. He could hear a few phrases.

"Alex Madden is here?"

"Yeah, and that's his brother over there!"

"The one in black with the rocker bag?"

"Hey, he's in my Calculus class."

"I didn't know he's Alex's brother.

"He's kinda cute don't you think?"

"Why isn't he in any of the frats like his brother?"

"Why isn't he in any of the sports teams?"

Jonathan walked faster, trying his best to ignore the people gossiping. He never wanted this and made it a point that he wouldn't be recognized. And yet with all that was happening such as the witnessing of Claire O' Hara's accident, and the gradual revelation of his association with Alex, he feared that his wish to remain unrecognized was all for naught.

"Jonathan, slow down. "Artemis said, walking fast to catch up to him. "Are you alright? You were a bit hostile to your brother back there."

"Wouldn't you be?" he asked.

"Not really." She admitted. "But that doesn't mean you should be mad at him. He is your brother, after all."

"You wouldn't know what it's like to be constantly called the little brother of Alex Madden." He said, as they left the building and walked across the lush campus grounds. They approached several benches under a massive tree and sat on them. Artemis could see that it wasn't just the notoriety or the incident at the road that was bothering him; it was something else.

"Why do I have a feeling there's more to this?" she asked him as he sat on the bench and lowered his head. "Look, I understand you don't want to talk about it. And that's fine with me. But at the very least, don't get mad at your brother. Or hate him for that matter"

"Artemis, I don't hate my brother. I actually love him very much." He began. "But, if you grew up being constantly known as the brother of someone who was basically a superstar, there's a lot of implied expectations to live up to."

"I don't see you doing that." She said. "In fact, I think you're great in your own way. So, why are you really mad at your brother?"

He felt his heart skip a beat when she said that. He had never had anyone tell him that before. He never had...someone truly and genuinely care about him. He looked at her and took a deep breath and replied. "I'm a very proud and independent kind of guy."

"Okay and that's a good thing." Artemis said as she settled back on the bench.

"So when I applied for Berkeley, I really wanted to see if I could get in on my own." He continued. "I was worried at first because I wasn't really proactive in high school. So the odds of me getting into Berkeley were sort of slim. But then I was accepted and I was happy."

"As you should."

"But it was only when I was having my first day orientation that I found out the real reason I got in. It was because Alex spoke to admissions right after I sent in my application." He replied, a wave of betrayal slowly flooding as he spoke. "They only accepted me because I was his little brother and not because of my abilities or anything."

"So you're a Legacy?" Artemis asked.

"Yeah, and it's something I'd rather keep to myself." Jonathan said. "I know what other students will say about Legacies and how easy it was for them to get accepted. I don't like that at all. So I was mad at Alex for that."

"Jonathan, you shouldn't be mad." She said. "Maybe he was just trying to help."

"That's the thing!" He bellowed, nearly startling Artemis. "I never asked for his help. I wanted to prove that I could make it on my own without any help whatsoever. I wanted to prove that my own abilities would be enough to let me attend Berkeley. Instead...I'm...I'm not so sure anymore."

"Have you ever told him how you felt about it?" she asked.

"He wouldn't understand, Artemis." He replied sadly. "And frankly, I don't think he knows what it's like. Being constantly compared to him, being hounded by frat boys and jocks to join their group, teachers asking you how your brother is faring, girls only liking you because of your famous brother..."

He stopped at the last sentence feeling a bit embarrassed at what he said. He had never before told anyone about his many frustrations growing up. He even remembered how he used to crush on a pretty girl who was a bit older than him. When he finally confessed his feelings to her, he was met with the hard truth that she only liked him because she wanted to get closer to Alex. He had known heartbreak and frustration in that one moment of his life. And now with what happened to Claire O' Hara, he felt he was partially responsible for her decision to make a bargain with the Lady on the Horse.

"I'm sorry." He quickly said. "That...that didn't come out right."

Artemis looked at him and then held his hand, and for the first time since that day, Jonathan felt his once broken heart beat again. This time, for Artemis. "You know." She began. "For the record, I didn't like you because of your brother. I like you because you're different from the other guys. That and you enjoy the mundane things in life like coffee, jazz and rain."

"Thanks, Artemis." He said, gripping her hand gently and looking at her. "You must think I'm a pathetic guy who has issues."

"Not really." She replied. "I just think you're a regular nerd."

He laughed at her remark, feeling almost better. But there was still that lingering sense that he was partially responsible for Claire O' Hara's death. Regardless, he thanked Artemis for being there and decided to focus on their search for the source of this strange game.

****

Nostalgic would be the proper word to describe what Alex was feeling, as he visited the imposing structure of the Sigma Chi Fraternity House. He recognized the vine covered brick walls, the large oriel windows, the gabled roofs and the trimmed bushes and topiaries.

'Nothing has changed with how the house looks,' he thought to himself as he walked to the front door. He heard excited sounds coming from behind the door. "Well, except for the new occupants." He chuckled as he reached for the knocker.

"Well, well, well. If it isn't Alex 'The Stampede' Madden!" A voice called out. Alex turned to see a football suddenly flying towards him with an almost uncanny speed. He turned around and caught the football with ease and smiled.

"What happens when you frighten the wildebeests?" Alex called out as he threw the football in the direction of the voice. "You get the Stampede!"

The football flew and another man caught it in his arms. He walked towards Alex and said. "Damn, you still got the Olympian's throw!" He was as tall as Alex with a similarly athletic build. He had blonde hair and hazel eyes. He was dressed in a casual attire consisting of a pair of blue jeans, a shirt and a Berkeley varsity jacket.

"Eric Douglas, you haven't changed a bit." Alex said as he held his hand out to shake Eric's. The two men looked at one another before giving each other a hug, as was customary of former Sigma Chi members.

"So what brings Sigma Chi's famous fellow back to its hallowed halls?" Eric asked in a grandiose manner.

"I was invited back by the University President." Alex replied. "I still don't know why, but it does give me a break from all the NFL games of the season." He then added. "And you?"

"Oh, I'm the House Director of Sigma Chi." Eric replied. "I'm taking care of our boys. Like how old Terry used to do when we were here before."

"Whatever happened to old Terry?" he asked

"Moved up north to Oregon." Eric replied. "He always wanted to live near the river and do some fly fishing. Want to come inside?"

"Yeah, sure." Alex replied as Eric opened the door and invited him in. The interior of the Sigma Chi fraternity house was a unique blend of masculine and classic elements, with large paneled walls and framed portraits of past fraternity presidents; Alex would even see his own portrait. There were chairs lined up along the hallway, and several boys could be seen moving around in each of the house's many rooms.

A boy was playing with some other boys in the hallway as they were approaching Eric and Alex. He stopped and greeted Eric. "Hello, Mr. Douglas." He said.

"Hello, Ted." Eric said. "Why are you running in the hall?"

"We're practicing for the next flag football so," Ted looked at Alex and dropped the football he was holding. "Holy shit! You're...you're..."

"Watch your language, Ted." Eric reprimanded. But Ted ignored Eric's reprimand and continued to gawk at Alex. "....You're Alex the Stampede!"

One could only imagine just how exciting it was for the Sigma Chi boys to meet a former fraternity president, let alone a celebrated college superstar like Alex Madden. It had been ingrained in them, from the moment they stepped inside the house, all of Alex's college exploits that, if put into pen and paper, would rival any typical college film story. One by one, Alex would hear the boys ask him various questions.

"Did you really win the Greek row games?"

"How did you earn the name, the Stampede?"

"Is it true you were the youngest quarterback in the history of the university?"

"Is it true you starred in an indie film by Jim Jarmush?"

"Alright you guys, give the man some space." Eric said as he tried to diminish the crowd of excited Sigma boys. "I assume you want to visit your old room?"

"Among other parts of the house." Alex replied. "Is anyone living in it?"

"No way." One boy said. "We left it unoccupied. It's the fraternity's way of honoring our most famous brother."

Alex chuckled as he began to walk up the stairs towards the living quarters. He walked to the last room at the end of the hallway and opened it. Just as the boy had said, the room was empty. It was orderly and clean. The wooden bed that he used to sleep on had been arranged with clean white bedlinen and fluffed up pillows. The closet stood against the wall next to the bathroom door, and the desk and chair were still against the window. He closed the door behind him and walked to the bed. He could see what looked like a series of tape residue, as well as square and triangle shadows on the wall.

'I used to hang my posters and the University flag here.' He thought fondly as he tapped on the wall. He thought about the posters of beautiful girls and musicians like Blink182, Nirvana, Green Day and Red Hot Chili Peppers that used to fill up the walls. Hard to believe it was 8 years ago since he first entered this room. There was a knock on the door, before it opened and Eric walked inside the room.

"This brings back memories." He said as he looked at the room. "Hey, Alex. Remember when we were still brand-new initiates? Remember when the seniors would have us gather outside our rooms and they'd do a raid?"

"What was the point of those raids, I wonder?" Alex asked.

"I don't know, some crazy initiation rite." Eric said as he sat on the chair. "But when you became President, you kind of stopped that tradition."

"Didn't see the need for it." Alex said as he walked around the room. "Do they still do the initiation rites?"

"Nah, everyone's following some guide rules the University council set, ever since the whole rape and brutal hazing allegations started over at the other fraternities." Eric said. "Speaking of everyone, they all know your brother's here on campus."

"And so?"

"They've been trying to get him to join them." He replied. "But it seems like he doesn't want to have anything to do with Greek Row."

"He's never been a fan I'm afraid." Alex said. "Even when I tried to tell him that Sigma Chi would be good for him."

"What does he want to be after college?" Eric asked.

"A sociologist, actually." Alex said.

"Nerd alert?" Eric teased, casting a teasing glance at Alex. "Well, did you hear about how he was a witness at an accident?"

"Mr. Hart mentioned something about that." Alex said. "I did ask Jonathan about it, but he doesn't seem to want to talk about it. He's sort of hostile at me right now."

"Why?" he asked.

'Why indeed?' Alex thought. He didn't really know why Jonathan was mad at him. Perhaps he had caught him at a bad time.

He walked to the window and said. "Hey, Eric. Think I could bother you for some coffee?"

"Sure, man." Eric replied. "Tell you what, I know the perfect spot to get the best coffee. Let me just get my coat and I'll meet you downstairs, 'kay?"

"Sure." Alex replied, his gaze fixed on the window as Eric walked out of the room, leaving him completely alone. Alex then closed the door, walked back to the desk and opened the bottom drawer. It was empty. Or at least that's what it looked like. He looked into the drawer and saw a small peg hole big enough for his finger to go through. He inserted his finger into the peg hole and lifted the drawer's floor to reveal a secret compartment. Inside the compartment was a small red notebook.

'It's still here,' he thought, picking up the notebook from the compartment and opening it. He looked through the written pages and thought about the days back when he wrote on them. How each page reminded him of something he should never forget.

He quickly pocketed the notebook in his jacket and began walking out of the room, when he suddenly heard something roll out of his desk and hit his foot. He looked down and saw a golden round bell. He picked it up and held it in his palm. At the same time, he glanced at his left hand and stared at an unusual ring on his finger. Somehow, he felt an almost uncanny and unnerving feeling; one he had never felt in such a long time.

****

UC Berkeley, 7 years ago.

Boys were sitting on the bleachers as the University's football coach paced in front of them, observing their faces and wondering whether these hopeful boys had what it took to make it into the team. Coach Paul Jones studied the roster of applicants on his clipboard. 'These were all freshmen,' he would think to himself. 'Not an ounce of potential in any of them. Or is there?'

"Alright boys." He said. "Football. An All-American pastime. I'm sure you played football in your respective high schools." He shook a finger at them. "Those were the minor leagues. This is the major league. You get into the team; I guarantee there will be agents who will scout for potential drafts for the Big Leagues."

There were excited murmurs coming from the boys as the coach began calling out the names. Among the hopeful boys was a young man with black hair and hazel eyes that were focused and determined. One of the other boys noticed him and said. "So, what are you hoping to get?"

"I'm sorry?" The boy with black hair replied.

"Are you hoping to be a quarterback or linebacker or long snapper?" The other boy asked.

"Oh, I'm hoping to be a quarterback." He replied. There came several snickering sounds coming from the rest of the boys. A burly looking African American then came forward and stood in front of the boy.

"What's your name, boy?" He asked.

The boy looked at him and replied. "Alex. Alex Madden."

"Well, Alex Madden. My name is Grover Johnson." The burly boy said. "And let me tell you this, boy, I've been a quarterback at my high school and I am getting that spot. You're better off with the other spots."

The rest of the boys chuckled in agreement with Grover Johnson. But Alex was unfazed. He was just like everyone else on the benches; all hopeful that they would get a spot. As each of the boys were called to demonstrate, Alex sat quietly in the benches, anxiously waiting. He reached for the ring on his finger and began to carefully twist it around.

"That your purity ring?" Another boy joked, noticing how Alex twisted it every now and then.

"Not really." He calmly replied. "It's.... sort of a good luck charm."

"Madden!" Alex nearly jumped as Coach Jones called his name out. He sprinted towards the coach. Coach Jones looked at Alex from head to toe. "Hmm...you have a good build, kid. But let's see how well you play." Coach Jones then had several members of the football team play a round with Alex. To his surprise, Alex was quite good. Very good in fact. He could see how Alex could easily maneuver in and out of the boys while holding on to the ball. He was also surprised at how fast he would charge towards the home field.

As soon as tryouts were over, the boys all sat by the bleachers and drank their water. Coach Jones then announced that results would be posted outside his office the following day. Alex picked up his towel and things. "Hey, boy!"

Alex turned to see Grover looking at him with a slightly impressed look. "Those were pretty impressive moves, boy." He said.

"Thanks...I think." Alex said.

"Ever played football before?" he asked.

"I did." Alex replied. "But just for fun."

"Well you got game." Grover said. "You look like you could outrun the team. Well, best of luck to you then." He picked up his things and walked away. Alex watched his retreating figure, all the while twisting the ring on his finger.

The next day, Coach Jones' results were immediately posted outside his office. The boys gathered around the list to see who made the cut. Grover Johnson's name was surely on the list. And one could only imagine just how thrilled he was. When Alex Madden walked towards the list, Grover gave him a somewhat smug look, expecting to see Alex disappointed.

"Whoa, I don't believe it." Grover would hear excited voices coming from behind. "Madden, you made the list! And you're quarterback!"

"What?!" Grover made his way to look at the list and sure enough, for the world to see, the typewritten name of Alex Madden was on top of his own. What's more, next to his name was the player role he would have. Quarterback. He got quarterback?!

"How in the world did you get the quarterback slot?" One of the boys asked. "No one can get the slot that easily?"

"You must have really impressed the coach." Another boy said. Alex remained silent and simply walked away from the office. He felt his heart swell with happiness as he looked at the ring on his finger.

"It really worked." He said to himself.

"Hey, Stampede!"

Eric's voice cut through Alex's thoughts as he quickly dropped the golden bell and opened the door. As he walked out of his old room, he heard the faint sound of ringing bells coming from outside of the window. He looked over his shoulder and saw in the distance, a strange dark figure standing beside one of the campus's large trees. But before Alex could get a good look at it, Eric called out to him. So he brushed it aside and walked out of the room, not noticing that the golden bell had slowly vanished.

****

Jonathan was listening intently to Dr. Lewis's lecture on how social behaviors vary with different cultures. He opened his textbook and took notes while listening to Dr. Lewis. He suddenly heard a few students talking and he managed to listen in.

"I heard Alex Madden is here."

"He's visiting?"

"I heard the university is planning something for him."

"What could it be?"

"Well he is pretty popular and one of the university's most famous alumni. Maybe they're honoring him with something."

"Wow, that is something."

"Gee, I would like that kind of legacy. To be famous and stuff."

"Yeah, not like that one hit one wonder, Claire..."

'It seemed that Claire was now being referred to as a one hit wonder.' Jonathan thought. The news of his brother's return seemed to have overshadowed her unfortunate death. Still, he did what he always did best and ignored anything that involved his brother.

And besides, the lecture of Dr. Lewis seemed very interesting. The social behaviors that were a norm in different cultures. Perhaps he could take a page from this and apply to his search for the Lady on the Horse. He then heard a ping from his phone. He looked under his seat and saw it was from Artemis. He read the screen and smiled.

Artemis: *"Hey, my uncle George is in town and he wants to have dinner with me. I asked if I could bring a friend and he said yes. So, want to have dinner with my uncle?"*

Jonathan remembered how his dorm neighbor, Milo Garnier, in a way, worshipped and idolized Artemis's uncle who was a famous historical writer of numerous books. He did promise Milo an autograph. And it would be a good distraction of sorts from the whole shock of seeing his brother on campus. But more importantly, it meant that he would see Artemis again.

He quickly texted back and after sending it, settled back in his seat, smiling as he looked forward to the dinner. He thought to himself. 'At least, even for a moment, I won't have to think about the Lady on the Horse. Or Alex for that matter.'

<u>Chapter 3</u>

Dr. Joseph Lewis was the kind of teacher who appreciated those who were interested in his class lectures. Sociology, in his own words, was never a permanent field of expertise. Society constantly changes their way of thinking and as such, understanding both past and present cultural practices is crucial to the study of sociology.

In his many years of educating and research, he had encountered many students and their different approaches to study. But of all the students, he was pleasantly surprised to find one who was particularly interested and focused.

In fact, it surprised him the most when the student in question came up to him after his lecture was over. Dr. Lewis was keeping his laptop and papers when he heard a voice ask. "Dr. Lewis, may I ask you something?"

He looked up to see it was Jonathan. "Why, Mr. Madden. Yes, what can I do for you?"

"I was wondering if I could ask you about a topic that I'm...researching on."

"Oh?" Dr. Lewis replied, closing his bag and slinging it on his shoulder. "And what topic would this be?"

"I'm trying to understand...why some people readily believe in...urban legend rituals." Jonathan said.

"Ah, I see." Dr. Lewis then asked Jonathan to walk beside him as they left the classroom. "Would this be related to my topic last week on fortune telling rituals across time?"

"Something like that." Jonathan said. They walked along the hallway, passing students who had gathered in small groups to discuss their week's homework. "I'm sure you know about those rituals like Bloody Mary and Charlie Charlie?"

"Ah, the quintessential 'Summon a spirit and it will answer all your questions and grant your wishes." Dr. Lewis said.

Jonathan nodded as he continued. "I want to know why people would believe that sort of thing works?"

"It all dates back to ancient civilization." Dr. Lewis replied. "If you look at mythology and historical understanding, you will recall the Ancient Greeks sought the god's favor by performing various rituals meant to appease them."

"But there are some Gods that demanded human sacrifices, right?" Jonathan asked.

"That is true." Dr. Lewis replied. "But as soon as society evolved and adopted rational thinking, the archaic practices were deemed unnecessary and often times, evil."

"But that doesn't tell me why people would believe that it works." Jonathan said. "What could they possibly think the outcome would be?"

"It's very simple, Mr. Madden." Dr. Lewis replied. "People want to believe. Throughout various societies and cultures, people want to believe in the abilities of things that they cannot see or comprehend. Things that can grant what is normally unattainable."

"So where does the whole supernatural aspect come in?" he asked.

"I would say around the time when Christianity became the dominant religion and the Church was established." Dr. Lewis said. "The leaders who, by virtue of knowledge, had declared that the pagan practices of ritualistic summoning were considered the works of the Devil. And it has been so ever since."

Jonathan took note of what Dr. Lewis said and then he thought about it. If the idea of summoning some supernatural force to grant wishes was as old as time itself, then how did it translate to various incarnations? Was it even possible that all of these versions were rooted from one singular source?

"If you don't mind my asking, Mr. Madden." Dr. Lewis began. "May I ask why you are interested in this topic? Is this related to the popular Lady on the Horse game I am hearing?"

"Uh…not really, no." Jonathan said, trying his best to hide the truth. "But, it would be a good…uh…topic for my thesis."

"I see." Dr. Lewis reached into his jacket pocket and pulled out a card case. "If you need more information about ancient societies and their practices, I can recommend an old friend of mine." He handed a card to Jonathan.

Jonathan looked at the card and read the name across. GEORGE ROSI. 'Wait!' he thought. 'Isn't this…' He looked at Dr. Lewis and said. "George Rosi? I was just invited to have dinner with him by his niece, Artemis."

"Yes, I've heard you and Ms. Rosi are quite close as of late." Dr. Lewis said. Jonathan looked away for a brief moment, a tinge of red appearing on his cheeks. "She's a very interesting young lady." Dr. Lewis continued. "She attends my mythology culture lectures every Wednesday. Very bright girl and a promising Historian."

"Yeah, she's really something." Jonathan added casually.

"I hope you won't do anything to make her upset, Mr. Madden." Dr. Lewis said. "Her uncle and I are very good friends and I hate to see her sad."

'What was Dr. Lewis implying?' Jonathan thought. 'Was he suggesting I would hurt Artemis?' She's someone I like very much.

I'd be upset if anyone made her upset. So why was Dr. Lewis saying that. "I understand, Dr. Lewis." Jonathan said. "But you have my assurance that I won't...upset Artemis."

He checked his watch for the time. "Thank you again for giving me a little insight on my research, Dr. Lewis." He said. "If ever I need more info..."

"You only have to ask." Dr. Lewis finished. "And speaking of research, are you still interested in my researcher's program?"

****

Jonathan Madden could hardly believe the good news he got. Dr. Lewis had accepted his application as a research assistant in his program. He thought about all the possible topics and subjects they would research on, the many trips and lectures he would attend and so on. Just thinking about them made him very happy. So happy that he nearly forgot that he had a dinner date to get to.

He picked up his towel and headed towards the bathroom. Placing the towel on the rack, he stepped into the shower and turned on the knob. The water gently splashed on Jonathan's body as he sang a little tune to pass the shower time.

"Ride....a cock horse to Banbury Cross....To see a fine lady...upon a white horse. Rings on her fingers and bells on her toes and she shall have music wherever she goes..."

He stopped for a bit when he suddenly realized that he was singing the old rhyme that his mom often sang to him when he was little. 'Why was I singing that rhyme again?' He thought to himself. 'And in the first place, why did that particular rhyme have such a strong impact on him.' He turned off the shower and went to the sink to shave.

The mirror had fogged up from steam of the shower. Jonathan placed his palm on the glass and began to wipe it. He picked up the shaving cream and smeared a generous amount onto his face, then picked up his razor and began to shave his face. Slowly, he swept the razor across the small prickly field of facial hair, taking care not to cut himself.

"AH!" He flinched as the blade nipped his skin. He set the razor back on the sink, washed his face and reached for the strip of tissue. He then lifted his head to look at the mirror, but was met with a frightening sight.

In the reflection of the mirror was the unmistakable face of Claire O' Hara staring at him; her face bloodied and bruised and in complete agony. "Help me...." She seemed to be saying. Jonathan was speechless. How could he help her?

"I...I don't know how." He replied. Why the hell was he suddenly talking to the reflection of a girl who was dead? Claire's reflection looked at him with such a deep and mournful look. 'This can't be real,' he thought. 'Why am I seeing this?'

He then noticed that her face began to contort and melt away. At the same time the room began to grow dark. Jonathan started to look around the small bathroom, before looking back to the mirror and seeing the Lady standing right behind him!

He looked over his shoulder and saw nothing. He turned back again to the mirror and gasped as the Lady stretched her hand out of the glass mirror and grabbed Jonathan by the neck!

He started to gasp for air, as he held on to the Lady's eerily smooth hand and tried to pry them away from his throat. However, it seemed that the more he struggled, the tighter the Lady's hand grew on his neck. Jonathan began to drift in and out as he gasped for air. He turned his gaze towards the Lady's veiled visage. He could see, beneath the silken layers of fabric, frightening red eyes looking at him.

Finally, he loosened his grip on the Lady's hand as he closed his eyes and began to lose consciousness. At the point where everything seemed to be getting enveloped in darkness, he heard a familiar voice call out. "Hey, what the hell happened to you!?"

Dick had entered their dorm room and noticed small puddles of water on the floor. He heard the sound of flowing water coming from the bathroom. As he walked towards the door, he could see water seeping through the door. He opened it to find Jonathan sprawled on the soaked floor. Dick, in a panic frenzy, bent down and began to pat his cheek to wake him up.

"Yo, Jonny boy!" he cried out, patting each side as he did. "What happened? Are you okay? Wake up!"

Slowly, Jonathan began to stir and wake up. He sat up and looked at Dick, whose face was completely paralyzed with shock. "Dick, is that-?" He stopped midsentence as he looked around the bathroom. "Dick, did you see that woman?"

"What woman?" he asked. "Wait, are you having a girl in here?"

"What? No, I'm not. What the hell!" Jonathan said as he got up and turned off the faucet.

"Whoa, what happened to your neck?" Dick said.

Jonathan looked at his reflection in the mirror and saw long red marks on his neck. 'He wasn't imagining it,' he would think to himself. He really did see her. But why?

"Hey man, what happened back there?" He would hear Dick ask again. It was the first time he heard Dick sound genuinely worried. He was never the type to be easily frightened. Then again, any rational thinking person would agree that seeing someone unconscious and sprawled on a wet floor would immediately alarm just about anybody.

"I...I slipped." Jonathan said.

"You slipped?" Dick repeated, eyeing him intensely. "Why did you slip?"

"Well, I lost my balance." Jonathan replied simply. "Anyway, thanks for...waking me." He walked out of the bathroom and towards his closet; with Dick looking at him. As he opened his closet and pulled out a clean shirt, he heard Dick ask. "So what did you mean when you asked 'Did you see that woman...?'

'Oh crap!' He thought. 'I wasn't thinking when I asked him that. What do I say?' He looked over his shoulder and replied. "Oh, I was probably having one of those daydreams that I thought were real."

He hoped that Dick would be foolish enough to believe his reasoning. After all, if he had told the truth of what he really saw, how exactly would Dick react? Most likely, he'd be called insane. Crazy. A nut job, just to name a few.

He looked at Dick's face and saw how it seemed to somehow relax. 'He bought it,' he thought. Dick let out a deep breath and said. "Dude, you know what I think?"

"What?" Jonathan asked.

"I think...you need to get out more often." He replied. "You've been studying too much, man. That's why you slipped." He patted Jonathan by the shoulder and added. "Man, if Alex Madden's little brother knew what happened to you, he'd probably get pissed at me!"

'That doesn't make any sense at all.' Jonathan thought. 'And why involve my brother one more time?' But at least he bought into it. He slipped into a pair of black pants and buttoned up his shirt. "Well, I'm heading out."

"Where are you going?" Dick asked.

"Oh, Artemis invited me to dinner with her uncle." Jonathan said. "So I'm heading out." He walked to the front door and was about to open it when Dick called out. "Hey, your bro's back on campus right? Think you can introduce me to him?"

Jonathan sighed and muttered, "If I have the time..." He opened the door and headed out. 'Or if I run into him, which is highly unlikely.' He made his way along the hallway and down the stairs towards the main door. He pulled out his phone and sent a message to Artemis asking her for the location of the restaurant.

'The Tavern by Mykonos. Looks like I'm having Greek.' He thought as he mounted his scooter and sped off towards the restaurant. As he drove along the school grounds, he saw what looked like a group of girls gathering around a small memorial in front of the girls' dormitory. He stopped for a moment and saw an easel displaying Claire O' Hara's various headshots and modeling photos, which had been set up at the entrance of the dorm. There were candles and letters and bunches of flowers strewn all over, with some of the girls stopping by to place some more offerings and flowers.

'Despite all that, she was still a student and she did have some friends.' He thought as he started the scooter and drove on, all the while thinking of what he had just seen back in the shower. 'Why did he see Claire in the mirror? Was it guilt that he couldn't help her? Or...was it something else?'

****

The Tavern by Mykonos was the premiere Greek restaurant in the whole city. Established by Greek immigrants, the Tavern boasted of a delicious menu of authentic Greek meals such as Gyros, Moussaka, Pansetta, and Baklava.

Jonathan had heard about the Tavern by Mykonos, but had never been one to try and dine there. For one thing, he wasn't the adventurous type and two, the prices were quite high. "Jonathan, there you are." He turned around to see Artemis dressed in a coffee colored tiered dress and a light blue jacket.

"Hi Artemis. Wow, you're wearing a dress." He said, looking at her from head to toe.

"Well, my uncle George always complains that I don't wear dresses often." She replied. "So every time he's here, I have to wear a dress at the very least."

"You look good in a dress." He said, noticing how her cheeks went slightly red at that comment. "Well, are we going in?"

"Yeah, oh and uh…" She started. "Umm…my uncle's inside at our table and he…. he said he also brought a guest with him…."

"That's fine with me." He said. "Besides, it would be great to meet your uncle. Dr. Lewis suggested I make his acquaintance for certain research topics."

"Right, you're in his Sociology program." Artemis said as they walked through the doors and wove through the crowded tables, towards a section in the restaurant where the tables had a view of the city. A man sat in one of the tables dressed in a full suit and tie. He looked to be in his late 50s with a streak of grey in his brown hair. He had olive tanned skin and a short, but bristly beard.

"Theios George!" Artemis exclaimed as she walked to the elderly man.

The man looked up and smiled as he got up and replied. "Agapití mou anipsiá, Ártemis." He walked over and hugged Artemis. Then he looked at Jonathan and asked. "And who is this young man before me?" Jonathan was quick to notice that he had a very thick Greek accent.

"Theios, this is my friend that I told you about." Artemis said as she held Jonathan by the arm. "This is Jonathan Madden. He's a Sociology major. Jonathan, this is my uncle, George Rosi."

"Please to meet you, Mr. Rosi." Jonathan said, holding his hand out.

"A very polite young man." George Rosi replied, shaking Jonathan's hand firmly. "My anipsiá has been telling me so much about you."

"Anipsiá?" Jonathan repeated.

Artemis quickly said. "Anipsiá means niece in Greek. Theios is uncle. I'm sorry, Jonathan. I forgot to tell you that we speak a mixture of Greek and English in our family."

"That's alright." He assured her. "Maybe I'll learn a little Greek after tonight."

"Come, come!" George Rosi said as he led the two teens to a table. "Let us wait for my guest. While waiting, order whatever you like." He called for a waiter, who came over and gave them the menus. Jonathan looked over the menu, wondering exactly what he would like.

"You should try the gyros." Artemis whispered. "They're really good."

"Alright." He said as he told the waiter his order. As soon as the waiter left, George Rosi then asked. "So, tell me Jonathan about yourself."

"Myself, sir?" he repeated.

"My Anipsiá tells me you are a dedicated student in Sociology." George said. "It is very rare for Artemis to speak highly of someone else."

"She talks to you about me?" he asked, glancing at Artemis' slightly beet red face. "Oh, well...I really wanted to be an author. But to be an author, I decided to study Sociology. And it's been a very interesting major."

"It is very rare to see young men interested in Sociology." George said. "Most men go for Engineering or even Political science."

"I'm not like most guys." Jonathan said, just as the waiter returned with their appetizers. Jonathan looked at the dishes set before him. There was a platter of feta and yogurt pitas, meatballs that Artemis said were called keftethakia, which were a delicious meal in its own and fried vegetable fritters called favokeftedes.

Jonathan took one of each and placed them on his plate. With his fork, he took a bite out of each of them. They were delicious. He had never tasted anything so uncanny and good. "How do you find it, young Jonathan?" George asked.

"It's very tart." Jonathan said. "But good. There's a lot of vegetables and dairy in these appetizers."

"We Greeks love our vegetables and the use of dairy is a staple." George said. "Olives are also part of the cuisine as they are-"

"An homage to how the olive tree is sacred to Zeus?" Jonathan said. George Rosi seemed pleased to hear that. Artemis looked at Jonathan and added. "I'm glad you could make it tonight, Jonathan."

"Well, let's say I have a good reason as well." He replied before addressing George Rosi. "Mr. Rosi, I was actually planning to reach out to you." Jonathan said. "I was referred to you by Dr. Lewis."

"Ah, Joseph Lewis?" he asked. When Jonathan nodded, George Rosi continued. "We are very good friends. What were you hoping to ask me?" Before Jonathan could reply, George got up and smiled. "Ah finally. You're a bit late, my young friend."

"I apologize, George." said a voice. "I had a previous engagement and we finished late."

Jonathan recognized the voice. But there was no way it was possible. He looked over his shoulder and saw...

"Alex?!" Jonathan exclaimed as he stared at the towering figure of his older brother dressed in a smart suit, and wielding a small bouquet of flowers.

In many instances in a person's life, coincidences happen on an almost daily basis. This could be exemplified when your mother and teacher are best friends or, in Jonathan's case, his older brother is invited to the same dinner as he was. He wanted very much, even for one night only, to not have to think about his brother. And yet, here he was, in his radiating glory and dressed to the nines.

Alex walked towards Artemis and said. "I hope your niece likes daisies." He presented the small bouquet to Artemis before noticing his brother. "Jonathan...oh this is a surprise. I didn't know you were acquainted with George."

"I just met him today." He replied, a slight hint of displeasure resonating in his voice. "His niece invited me to dinner."

"That makes sense." Alex said as he shook George's hand. "George, I'm sorry for being late. I hope my brother has kept you entertained."

"Brother?" George repeated as he looked at both Alex and Jonathan. "Ah, now I see the resemblance. What an uncanny coincidence, wouldn't you say?"

"It is." Alex said as he sat next to George. Artemis could see the same seething look across Jonathan's face. She leaned in and whispered to him. "Are you alright, Jonathan?"

Jonathan immediately softened up and said. "Not really. But I won't let this spoil tonight." He watched as George and Alex began to converse as though they had been very dear friends. "Did you know your uncle knew my brother?" he asked Artemis.

She shook her head. "Not that I was aware of."

"So, Artemis." Alex began, turning his focus towards Artemis, while George directed the waiter to serve the dinner. "I'd like to know how you and my brother met."

"Well...we sort of bumped into one another." Artemis said. "Literally..."

"He was listening to his music and didn't see you?" Alex asked, managing a stiff chuckle. Jonathan however, remained quiet and calm. Artemis continued. "Well he had a lot on his mind, I think. But it's okay. I'm glad he bumped into me."

'She was glad I bumped into her?' He thought to himself feeling his heart beat a little faster. "Well, that is a surprise indeed." Alex said. "I've never seen my brother take a keen interest in any girl."

"And what is that supposed to mean?" Jonathan asked.

"Well, ever since you were a kid, Jon you were always staying in Dad's library reading his books and listening to music." Alex said. "You weren't really interested in girls."

"That's because most of the girls who came to the house were dumb airheads." Jonathan said. "The only thing they cared about was…"

"Oh look, our dinner's here!" Artemis said as waiters appeared, bearing trays of the night's dinner. There was a dish of grilled on skewers, moussaka, a plate of cooked fish in lemon and oil dressing, yogurt dips, and a plate of baklava. Jonathan quickly quelled himself down from finishing his sentence. No use in spoiling the dinner with his statements.

"Well then, everyone dig in." George said as he began to serve everyone the skewers of grilled meat. Jonathan cut into his meat and took a bite. The spices and herbs mixed in the meat were simply divine.

"Aww! Grilled meat is my favorite!" He heard Artemis exclaim as she bit into her skewer. 'So it was her favorite. Maybe he could learn how to cook meat just like that…'

"So, young Jonathan." George started. "You mentioned there was something you were planning on telling me?" Jonathan swallowed his mouthful and nodded. "Well, I have this…uh…pet project of mine that I would need your expertise in."

"Oh, what is it about?" George asked.

"Well…it's about ancient societies and their rituals." He replied. "I want to get a further understanding on how it was practiced." George Rosi scratched his bearded chin and looked at Alex. "Correct me if I'm wrong. But did you once ask me the same question your brother is asking, my friend?"

'Alex asked George Rosi the same question?' Jonathan blinked. 'Why in the world would he ask that?' Alex looked at George and chuckled. "Oh yes, I did. It's a really interesting topic, Jonathan."

"Gee, I wonder what you could possibly learn from ancient cultures." Jonathan said. "And why did you ask about that?"

"Same reason." Alex said. "I was interested in ancient practices."

"You were a Civil Engineering major!" Jonathan said. "How can ancient societies interest you?"

"You'd be surprised." Alex replied. Jonathan was starting to feel his temper slowly rise, but at Artemis' subtle nudging, he calmed down. George Rosi then said. "Well, I'll be happy to share with you all that I know about ancient societies. Truth be told, it would be nice teaching another Madden."

'Great.' Jonathan thought. 'Once again, I'm just another Madden.' He continued to eat his dinner. On occasion, George Rosi would ask Jonathan about himself, but most of the time, he would chat with Alex. It wasn't all that bad, really. After all, he was getting to know Artemis in a way. And he still had George Rosi's promise to teach him all he can about ancient societies. They could be the root to the origin of Lady on the Horse.

"Theios, have you heard about this urban legend called The Lady on the Horse?" Artemis asked as she ate her baklava. Jonathan looked at her. Perhaps she read his mind and decided to ask her uncle. He wouldn't suspect his niece's innocent conversation starter. George Rosi drank his wine and replied.

"Unfortunately, no. Why? Is this another one of those bastardized stories?"

"Bastardized stories?" Jonathan asked. Before George could reply, Alex spoke. "It's where people add elements to a story to a point that its original source has long been forgotten."

"Well said, Alex." George said, complimenting him.

Jonathan muttered under his breath. "That was unnecessary." Artemis then continued. "But, Theios. You have heard of it, right? If you want a wish granted, all somebody has to do is visit a crossroad at midnight and wait for a beautiful lady on a horse."

George Rosi finished his wine, set the glass down and said. "The idea of having a wish granted by a lady on a horse is a story that is as old as the ancient Greek pantheon. You will recall the story of Orpheus and how he ventured into the underworld, and made a deal with Hades that he would be reunited with Eurydice."

"Yeah, I remember that story." She replied. "He could bring her back provided he didn't look behind before exiting the underworld. And he screwed that up."

"What did that story teach us?" he asked.

Alex then finished his wine and said. "George, may I?" George nodded and Alex continued. "That there are things in this world that come with a very, very high price. And it is a price that not many are willing to pay."

"Exactly." George said. "Then there are those stories like Faust, who supposedly had his wish granted by the devil in exchange for his soul. Regardless, my dear Anipsiá, they are cautionary stories that warn us that our choices have a profound effect on our lives. Which is why you must be very careful with the choices you make."

Jonathan who had been silent then asked. "But, do you think the Lady on the Horse legend is true?" There was stillness around the table. George then replied. "I personally think it's not true. It is a story that has, in my opinion, no proven origin whatsoever."

Then what exactly did Artemis and I see when we saw Claire get run over? Jonathan thought. Alex then cleared his throat and said. "Well, I'd like to change the topic, if it's alright with everyone? I have a very important announcement to make."

****

A year ago...

Jonathan was sitting in his room playing a game on his computer, all the while checking out the window for any sign of the mailman. He was nervous about something and he busied himself by playing a couple of levels on his computer game.

It had been almost three months since he submitted his applications to various colleges, and so far, not one of them had contacted him for an interview. He was starting to think that he wasn't good enough for those institutions. His door opened and Alex walked in. He set his bag down and pulled a chair close to Jonathan.

"What level is that?" He asked Jonathan.

"The part where Thrall has to fight Grom Hellscream." Jonathan said as he pressed several keys and made the characters move. "You're home early."

"Well, I won't be leaving until the end of the month." Alex said, eyeing the pile of games next to Alex's computer. He counted the games and said. "Hmmmm... and how many games have you played so far?"

"Just a couple.... maybe 6?" Jonathan replied.

"You're nervous about something." Alex said. "You normally play one game. But this is entirely a different thing. You're stressing about something."

"Well...it's the college applications." Jonathan said, removing his headphones and placing them on his desk. "I've applied to many colleges and none of them have contacted me."

"That's how it is." Alex said. "They usually start the shortlisting 4 weeks after. You have nothing to be nervous about." He then added. "Just out of curiosity, which universities did you apply to?"

He listened as Jonathan enumerated all the universities he applied to. His ears perked up when he heard Berkeley. "You applied to both Dad and my alma mater? Did you state your relation or anything?"

"No, because if I did, I would become a Legacy." Jonathan replied.

"Yeah and getting in will be a guarantee." Alex said. "You did state your relation to us, right?"

"No way." Jonathan said in a firm tone. "I want to get in on my own. I don't want to rely on you or Dad or anything. Anyone can get into Berkeley, even if they don't have a stellar academic record."

"There's nothing wrong with being a Legacy, Jonathan." Alex glanced at his brother's bookshelves and looked at the book titles. "And besides, Berkeley would be very lucky if they accepted you. You're a smart kid."

"I don't get why college applications always have those questions where they ask about your extracurricular activities." Jonathan said. "What's the point?"

Alex had always known that Jonathan was the type who avoided school activities involving large groups of people. He wasn't the athletic type or the overtly intellectual. And he was certainly the type who did not have any ambition. Or at the very least...confidence.

"Well, regardless." He heard Jonathan speak. "Whichever college I get in, I'll be content knowing that I got in on my own." He put his headphones back on and went on to play his game. "And I'll always have you, Alex. At least you believe that I can. Right?"

Alex nodded and replied. "Of course. I am your older brother after all. I'll always be proud of you."

The weeks turned into months and then one day, when Jonathan came home, he saw there was mail on top of the console table. He picked it up and walked to the living room, flipping through each envelope until he came across a thick, legal sized envelope with his name typed across it. He held it in his hand and his eyes quickly darted to the printed header. He couldn't believe who the sender was.

UNIVERSITY   OF   CALIFORNIA-BERKELEY, ADMISSIONS OFFICE.

It was the first application that responded. He quickly opened the envelope and took out the thick folded papers. 'This was it,' he told himself as he took a deep breath and unfolded the papers to read.

At the same time, Alex walked into the house and saw Jonathan staring at a piece of paper. "Hey Jon, what's that you got there?" He asked. Jonathan was completely ecstatic as he read the paper. "Hey-"

"It's from Berkeley." Jonathan muttered. "I'm...I'm in."

"Come again?" Alex asked.

Jonathan looked up and a smile crept across his face. "I'm in! I got into Berkeley!" He felt an immense swell of happiness course through his body. Upon hearing that his brother had gotten into Berkeley, Alex beamed and replied. "That's great. Congratulations!"

"I can't believe it!" Jonathan said. "I was actually worried at first because I was starting to think I had no chance at all. But this proves everything. I got in on my own. Do you know what this means?"

When Alex didn't reply, he continued. "This means I have what it takes! I'm gonna tell Mom and Dad!" He turned on his heel and headed towards his parents, leaving Alex alone in the living room. Alex smiled and then quietly reached for his phone and dialed a number.

"Hello?" He whispered into the phone. "Hey, it's me...Yes, he got the letter just now.... Thanks for taking his application into consideration. I hope it wasn't any trouble on your part...oh really? Thanks again.... Yes, he's a smart kid.... the department will be thrilled to have him.... alright. I'll see you and the president soon...thank you..."

__Chapter 4__

Jonathan had poured himself another glass of wine as Alex cleared his throat and began to speak. "I want to take this opportunity to let you know the reason why I have come back. The University is opening a new hall and they are naming it after me."

"Oh that is wonderful news." George Rosi said as he shook Alex's hand. "Congratulations, my friend."

"Thank you." He said. Then turning his gaze to his brother, he added. "I would be so thrilled if you could come, Jonathan."

"Gee, how could I pass up the opportunity to attend a ceremony glorifying my older brother's achievements?" Jonathan said in a slightly sarcastic manner as he emptied his wine glass. The table had grown silent. Artemis busied herself with drinking a little wine while George ordered more baklava. Alex stared at Jonathan and for the first time since they entered the restaurant, both brothers stared at each other with a deep and almost uncertain feeling. Alex looked at Jonathan's somewhat stony and, for lack of a better description, annoyed face. Jonathan on the other hand, looked at Alex's scrutinizing face.

"How about I order some more baklava?" Artemis said, trying to ease up the tension on the table. "We haven't tried the-"

"Is there something on your mind, Jon?" Alex said as he stared at Jonathan. "Got something bugging you?"

"Why would you think that, Alex?" Jonathan asked in a drawling tone. "There's nothing bugging me at all."

'I'm not an idiot, Jonathan.' Alex thought as he settled back in his seat. "Oh, I'm sure there's something on his mind. I'll just have to wait until he cracks." Noticing George Rosi's confused look, he added. "It's a game we used to play as kids. And every time we play that game, Jonathan always lost."

"What's that supposed to mean!?" Jonathan barked, furrowing his eyes and frowning at Alex; Artemis switched between nervously eating a piece of baklava and gently tugging at Jonathan's sleeve.

"I'm just saying that ever since we were little, you were always so obvious when there was something troubling you." Alex said. "Eventually, I'll figure it out and you'll tell me."

"Oh sure, you'll figure it out." Jonathan said, folding his arms. "Cause you're Alex Madden and you always get everything..."

SLAM!

Jonathan was unfazed as Alex slammed his hands on the table and glared at his brother. Immediately, all eyes were on their table as the other diners looked at them. George slowly got up and said. "Now, now my friends. There is no need for..."

"George, I apologize for our outburst just now." Alex said through gritted teeth. "Will you please excuse me and my brother as we talk in private?"

"Of...of course..." George said. "It's no trouble."

'Typical.' Jonathan thought as he wiped his lips with his napkin and placed it on the table as he got up from his seat. Artemis quickly held him by the wrist as if asking if he was going to be alright. Jonathan gave her an assuring look as his brother walked over to him and gestured him to follow him to the men's room. 'This always happens whenever we argue.' He thought as he followed Alex to the room. Lately, it seems that we have been arguing.

****

Six months ago....

Jonathan sat in the passenger seat of the Jeep, as he and Alex drove along the road towards the University of Berkeley. Behind them, sitting in the back seat, were boxes full of Jonathan's things that he would use in the dormitories, and two luggage cases filled with his clothes and shoes. "You nervous, Jon?" Alex asked as he watched Jonathan stare out of the car and into the cityscape.

"Well, I'm going to be away from everyone for an entire year." He replied as he clutched his backpack. "It's gonna be weird for me not having Mom's home cooked meals waiting for me when I get home."

"Yeah, you're gonna have to get used to the college diet." Alex said as the Jeep braked at a stop light. "If you're running late for class, a granola bar is your best friend until free period. And if you really need something to get you going, instant cup noodles with some boiled eggs!"

"Alex, I think between the two of us, I would already have an idea on what to eat when I'm there." He said, chuckling at his brother. Even if his older brother meant well, Jonathan was a self-proclaimed independent guy who could survive even an earthquake.

He was still reeling from finding out that he was accepted at his brother's alma mater. He knew that applying to an institution like Berkeley was difficult and hard. Applications were scrutinized and as far as he was concerned, he was the kind of guy who did not have "school spirit", and was not really involved with the various school clubs that fit the mold of a typical Berkeley student.

"I still can't believe I got in." He said. "I mean, I know getting into Berkeley is tough."

"It would have been easier if you just stated who you were related to." Alex said as the stoplight turned green. "Legacies can easily get in."

"Alex, I'll say it again. I don't like being a Legacy." Jonathan said, suddenly looking at him. "Especially if it's you."

"And what is that supposed to mean?" Alex said.

"What else?" He said. "I'm not really comfortable with being known as your little brother. I'd rather just have a normal experience without anyone harping about you, and how I ought to be more like you."

"Who keeps telling you that?" Alex asked.

"It's sort of implied." Jonathan muttered. "No one really takes me seriously." He was still thinking about Ashley, the girl from his class who visited him at home. Ashley, who was his project partner. Ashley, with whom he felt the first pangs of love. Ashley, who had broken his heart when she told him she only liked his brother.

"Is this coming from that girl?" Alex asked, eyeing his brother's slightly melancholic look.

"No..." Jonathan replied turning a faint shade of beet red.

"Don't lie." He said as they drove along the shop-lined streets. "You're thinking about that girl, aren't you?"

"Was it that obvious?"

"It's all over your face." Alex stopped the car in front of a small coffee shop. "Come on, let's have some coffee. I'll introduce you to this place." He unbuckled his seatbelts and got out of the car. Jonathan followed in suite and watched as his brother walked down a set of stairs leading to a door in the basement of a building. He noticed a sign that read 'Underground Brew' in a stylized script.

He then got a whiff of freshly brewed coffee beans permeating from behind the door. "Is that-?" He started. Alex smiled and opened the door. "Come on in." Jonathan cautiously walked inside and found himself in a small coffee shop with industrial style tables and chairs arranged against the exposed brick wall. Jonathan sat at a table located in a far corner, in between framed posters, while Alex walked to the counter to order their drinks.

"Well, well if it isn't Alex Madden." The barista said. "How you been, man?"

"Doing well, thanks Kyle." He replied. "Just stopping by for some good old brewed coffee with my brother, before heading to the University."

The barista, Kyle, looked at Jonathan and gave a small nod of approval. "Wow, that's your brother? I bet all the girls would go nuts when they see him."

"Nah, he's not really into that. "Alex replied.

"Ah, a rebel then." Kyle said. "And will he be joining your old fraternity?"

"I'll try and talk him into joining." He replied. "He'll need a friend or two if he wants to survive Berkeley." Alex went on to order two cups of brewed coffee and some pastries, before walking back to the table where Jonathan sat.

"You took a while." Jonathan said, looking over Alex's shoulder. "Friend of yours?"

"This is my favorite coffee shop outside of campus." Alex said. "So, I'm sort of a regular here." Kyle the barista arrived shortly after, placing the brewed coffee and pastries on top of the table before heading back to the counter. "So, if ever you need some good old brew coffee, this is the place."

Jonathan picked up his cup and took a small sip. 'He wasn't kidding,' he thought as he stared at the steaming drink. It was so good. "You know I don't like special treatment, Alex." He started. "So I hope the baristas won't do anything like ...oh I don't know...slip in extra shots of espresso every now and then."

"They won't." Alex said as he drank his cup of coffee. Then after taking a bite out of his pastry, he added. "Though there is something I have been meaning to ask you."

"And that is?"

"Have you ever considered joining my old fraternity?" he asked.

Jonathan sighed and replied. "Now, Alex..."

"Look, before you say anything." Alex began. "Let me just say that joining a fraternity isn't really that bad. You will have perks and a profound presence in the school, and when you graduate, you are guaranteed lucrative positions."

"I'm not really into fraternities, Alex." Jonathan said "It's not really my scene."

"But, you'll be able to breeze through college with a fraternity." Alex said, enumerating the many benefits his brother would have. "And you'll easily get in because you're my brother."

Jonathan suddenly looked at his older brother as though Alex had said something he should not have. He sipped his cup of coffee and after taking a deep breath, said. "Alex, I appreciate the gesture. But like I said before, I want to get through college on my accord. Not because you're my brother. I mean, it was great that I got accepted without them knowing I'm your brother. But I don't want to follow what you did."

"I see." Alex said softly. "I was just trying to…"

"I know, Alex." Jonathan leaned back against the backrest of the chair and folded his arms. "I'm sorry if I'm arguing with you."

"It's fine." Alex looked at his brother. The two brothers sat in complete silence as they finished their coffee and pastry. Jonathan had to admit; he had never pegged his college superstar brother to enjoy coffee in a shop that looked as though it were frequented by artists and poets.

After thanking the baristas, the two brothers got back into the car and headed towards the university. Alex looked at Jonathan and then said. "Regardless, I'm proud of you, you know."

"Why?" he asked

"Well…because I know you always do your best in whatever you do." He replied. "And I know you will do great in Berkeley."

"Thanks, Alex." Jonathan said. Then he spied something on his brother's finger that he had not seen before. Or at the very least, something he was sure his parents had never given him. "By the way, Alex, where did you get that ring?"

Alex looked at his hand and glanced at the ring on his little finger. Jonathan could see that it was an unusually luxurious looking ring. It was a small golden band that had an emerald stone surrounded by small diamonds. "That looks really expensive." Jonathan said "Did Dad give it to you?"

Alex shook his head. "Mom?" Jonathan suggested. Again Alex shook his head. "Well, where did you get it?"

"I…I got it…from a friend." Alex said.

"Really?" Jonathan looked at it. "It looks expensive. Must be some rich friend you have. Why did your friend give it to you?"

"It's between the two of us." He replied as they slowly entered the gates towards the University complex. Jonathan looked out through the window, his eyes taking in the beauty and splendor of the University of California-Berkeley. Alex watched as his brother marveled at the university complex, slightly looking away as though to hide a terrible secret.

****

Six months doesn't change the bond siblings have; at the very least it often strengthens one's relationship. But that was not the case for Alex and Jonathan as they walked towards the al fresco dining area of the restaurant. In truth, there was a deep anger inside Jonathan and Alex was quite oblivious to it. Or rather, he had never considered the small gestures Jonathan made.

Once they were far away from earshot, Alex started the conversation. "Alright, Jon. What's been bugging you?"

"Nothing is bugging me at all, Alex." Jonathan replied in a sarcastic tone as he folded his arms and leaned against the walls of the restaurant. "Are you trying to pull off the famous 'Alex solves everything' routine? Cause that's not going to work."

"You clearly have something on your mind." He frowned. "You might as well spit it out!"

"Why don't you just mind your own business, Alex?" Jonathan snapped. "You don't see me going up in your biz."

"Not until you tell me what's bugging you right now!" Alex said. "Ever since I came back, you're either avoiding me or you're irritated with what I do. What is wrong, Jonathan?"

"God, you are so pushy!" Jonathan glared at Alex, a frown slowly forming across his face. "Fine! Do you want to know what my problem is, Alex?!"

"Yes, I want to know!"

"My problem is you!" Jonathan barked like a dog finally baring his fangs at his enemy. Alex blinked as Jonathan spoke the words. Jonathan's problem ...was him? He stared down at his little brother and said. "And what is that supposed to mean?"

"Dammit, you are so full of yourself!" There was a sense of anger swelling up inside Jonathan, as though he had been containing years of repressed resentment. As far as he could remember, he had always hated being under his brother's shadow. Though it normally didn't offend him, and he had rather gotten used to it, the fact remained that by association to his brother, Jonathan had gotten preferential treatment. Something he was never fond of.

"Do you have any idea what it meant to me when I got into Berkeley?" Jonathan spat out. "What it meant for me to get in without any association whatsoever? It was like...they saw something in me. Something that didn't have anything to do with school involvement or any of that."

"Yes." Alex said. "And you know how proud I am of you that you got in. So I don't see how that has anything to do with-"

"You're proud of me!? That's a laugh, coming from you." Jonathan said. "That's a laugh...coming from a liar!"

"Now hold on there. Jon!"

"I found out that the real reason I got in was because you called the admissions office." Jonathan glared at his brother as the words stung him like a branding iron. He had kept this pain, this betrayal if one would describe it, to himself. "Do you deny doing that?"

"Jon, I was only-"

"DO YOU DENY IT!?"

Alex let out a deep sigh and looked away. "I don't deny what I did. But you have to understand, I was only looking out for you, like an older brother would." He then added. "But do you have any idea how tough it is to get into Berkeley on your own? "

"I had to try at least." Jonathan couldn't believe what Alex was saying. How could he say it was tough? He and his father had gotten in without any problems or anything. "And even if I didn't get in, there were other options. And what's really bugging me is the fact that you did this behind my back and went on as if nothing happened."

"Jon, I just wanted you to get in." Alex said. "But with your application, there was no possibility of you getting in." He suddenly stopped as he saw Jonathan's face slowly turn red with anger and fury. He had finally said it and he had not realized it.

"Mind explaining to me why my application couldn't possibly get me accepted, exactly?" Jonathan slowly clenched his hands into fists and waited for his brother to respond.

Alex stared at him from head to toe. It seemed as though there was no use denying or hiding the reason. After all, he only had good intentions for his brother. And at the very least, his brother ought to understand. "Do you want to know why?" he asked.

"I'm asking." Jon fired back. Around the same time, the diners who had been staying in the al fresco area had started to overhear the conversation between the two brothers and not wanting to be involved of sorts, quietly proceeded to leave. "Well?"

"Fine." Alex then said. "Berkeley will never accept students whose applications are not up to their standards. Good grades aren't enough. They want a student who is involved completely. And you don't fit the bill at all. So what choice did I have? I wanted you to have the best and....."

"So, you didn't think I could do it after all." Jonathan said. "Is that what you mean to say? That I'm not cut out for it?"

"Wait, that's not what I-"

"That is EXACTLY what you mean." Jonathan said, slowly loosening his fists and looking at his brother with a disappointed and angry look. "And here I thought my own brother believed in me. When all along, he just wanted his legacy to go on and on and on...What a fool I was..." And with that he turned on his heel and began to leave.

"Where are you going?" Alex asked.

"I'm going back inside." Jonathan replied. "I just can't look at you right now, knowing that you will never realize what a disappointment you really are to me." And with that he walked back inside, leaving Alex behind in the al fresco dining room.

Jonathan closed the door behind him and saw Artemis standing right in front of him. He looked at her, slowly thinking of what had happened earlier. Had he completely embarrassed himself in front of her and her uncle? Had he left a rather unsightly impression? More importantly, did she think differently of him?

"Were you standing there all this time?" he asked. She nodded. "Then you probably heard everything." He looked away and said. "I must have embarrassed myself big time. I didn't want my anger to get the best of me and m-"

He was abruptly cut off when Artemis wrapped her arms around him and gave him a rather reassuring hug. "Artemis?"

"It's alright." She said. "Don't apologize. Theios kinda had an inclining that you both needed to air out some issues."

"He's not mad at me? Or at you for bringing me over?" he asked.

"Not in the least." She said as she looked at him. "Actually, he likes you and has this funny idea that I should spend more time with you." 'He likes me?' He thought to himself as he looked at Artemis' smiling and reassuring face. Even after?

There was something about the way Artemis looked at him that in a way, gave him a sense of gratitude. There was at least something he had that his brother couldn't possibly deny of him. Here was a girl who he liked very much and who understood him completely. It was something that even the famous Alex Madden couldn't possibly have.

****

Alex watched as his brother turned on his heel and left him all by himself. He sat in one of the al fresco dining chairs and let out a disappointed sigh. He had never meant to hurt Jonathan and in a way, he had a right to be angry. He had always known his brother to be independent and to not rely on people for help. Was it not evident when he submitted his application and chose to omit the fact that he was related to two Berkeley alumni? Was it not enough for him to see how much his brother wanted to be his own person? Was it not enough for him?

"After this, Jonathan is never going to forgive me." He said grimly to himself. "I better make it right. Somehow."

Suddenly, he noticed fog slowly begin to appear and set in. He looked up at the sky to see if there were any rain clouds forming. The sky was clear and yet there were many stars that appeared. Alex wondered where the fog was coming from. It was so thick that it covered the surrounding buildings and streets. Alex got up and tried to make his way through the fog and back inside the restaurant. But with a thick fog that made it hard for anyone to find the right way, he was practically walking around in a blind path.

He wondered where the door to the main restaurant was and tried to grab for the handle blindly, but all he could feel was more fog. He walked for what seemed like a few minutes until he could see a tall shape in the distance. Walking quickly, he soon came to what looked like a crossroad with a gnarled tree in the center, its branches outstretched like bony fingers.

But this was no ordinary crossroad as Alex stared at the tree. He knew what this place was. After all, he had only been here once. He looked around the crossroads and for a brief moment, there was an eerie silence that he hoped he would never encounter again.

Suddenly, there came a familiar clip clopping sound of hooves in the distance. Alex looked towards the direction of the sound and sure enough, to both his horror and disbelief, he could see a large white horse slowly trotting towards him.

He could see the magnificent trusses of platinum and wheat hair on its head and neck, and leather muzzle on its person. Astride the horse on a jewel encrusted saddle was the delicate figure of a woman dressed in layers of silk and ivory. The same layers of silk and ivory partially covered her face, and were adorned with a tiny trim of gold. On her hands were bangles and rings of different styles and sizes adorning her delicate fingers. Rows of bells on golden chains wrapped around her ankles and toes.

The horse stopped in front of Alex and the veiled lady glanced at him. Alex looked at her and let out a sigh. "I have not forgotten my gratitude to you, dear lady." He said. "All that I am, I owe to you."

"And what success you have indeed." The lady responded in an ethereal tone. "Is it everything you had hoped for when you made the wish?"

"In a way, but..." Alex started as he felt a quiver crawl up in his throat. "I wished to leave a legacy unlike any other."

"And soon, you will." The lady said as she gently pulled on the reins of the horse's muzzle, gesturing him to start moving. "And when you have what you wished; I shall be back...to collect..."

With that, the horse trotted away, taking his mistress into the darkness. Alex blinked and started to chase after her. "Wait, what do you mean...collect?" he called out. But before he could get an answer, he found himself back in the restaurant by the main door. Unsure of what happened just now, Alex quickly opened the door and returned to the main dining room.

****

Jonathan had returned to his dorm and gotten into the shower. He had apologized to George Rosi for the scene he had caused and quickly left, avoiding Alex as he sat back on the table. As he drove on his scooter, he would get calls and messages from Alex. But he was not in the mood to talk or even reply to him. In one sitting, he had let out all that he had felt against his brother.

The months of being associated as Alex Madden's brother had taken its emotional toll on Jonathan. He had always brushed off the implied expectations from both teachers and students alike. He had even ignored the fact that girls would only talk and flirt with him just for the opportune chance to speak with Alex. He had ignored all of that because it didn't matter to him one bit.

But the pain of realizing that he was only in Berkeley because of Alex's interference and disbelief in his brother's own ability to get accepted was, in essence, the straw that broke the donkey's back.

He sighed sadly as the water gently hit his body, rinsing away whatever emotion he had that night. He knew that he could never hope to forgive Alex. Not after what he had learned and said. But, deep down, he still loved his brother. Perfection and all. Perhaps deep down, he truly admired his brother. But was too much of an independent to even acknowledge it.

He got out of the shower and wrapped a towel around his body. He went to his bed and saw that his phone had more missed calls and messages from Alex. He frowned for a bit and ignored them. "Not now." He said to himself. "Not tonight. Not yet that is." He pulled on his shirt and shorts and sat on his desk. He opened his laptop and began to browse the internet.

He glanced at his notebook where he had scrawled down many notes on the Lady on the Horse. He had nearly forgotten about his search for the truth about the legend. As fantastic as the story went, he was more than convinced that there was a deep-seated root to the story itself and why so many would attempt to call on her for wishes.

He could still remember the last inaudible words Claire mouthed to him before being taken away by the Lady on the Horse. 'Help me,' she said. But how could he help her? Why should he help her? He then heard his laptop sound. He looked to see it was Artemis calling. He smiled and then clicked on the accept button.

"Hey." He said as Artemis appeared on a popped-up window. He could see that she was also dressed for bed. "What's up?"

"Just checking in on you." She said, propping her head on her hands. "How you doing?"

"I'm fine. Could be worse. I might even just stay in bed because I feel sick." He chuckled.

"We can't have you feeling sick." She giggled. "But seriously, how are you?"

"Well, I let it all out." Jonathan said. "I let Alex have it. And he didn't seem to take it too well."

"Well, perhaps it's because it's finally biting him in the ass." Artemis said. "I mean, I'd be mad too if I found out my brother went behind my back and did something he wasn't supposed to." She reached for a glass of water and drank it. "He tried calling you after you left."

"I know." Jonathan replied. "I just don't want to talk to him yet. I mean, I'm still mad at the fact that he won't even apologize for what he did."

"I'm sure he meant well, Jonathan." Artemis said. "Getting into Berkeley really is hard. I'm sure he just wanted to help."

"He just wanted to help himself, Artemis." He said. "It would be another notch to his success. Alex Madden getting his little brother into Berkeley in order for his legacy to live on." At least, that's what he perceived in his anger. "But it was what he said that just..."

"I know..." She said, knowing all too well what she had heard. "But you know, what he said isn't true. I mean, yes, it is difficult. But you're still doing what you can and proving to everyone that you don't need exemplary school credentials to be here. You're already doing well in school."

"I know and I appreciate you reminding me, Artemis." Jonathan said, looking at her with a deep and almost loving gaze. She smiled back at him and said. "You know, Theios really likes you. He was wondering why we were interested in the Lady on the Horse legend."

"Didn't he say it was a bastardized version of some story?"

"Oh yes." She nodded. "But it sort of piqued his interest into looking at some of the stories associated with the Lady on the Horse. Maybe he could find the original version."

"All I know is that it has something to do with that old nursery rhyme." Jonathan replied. "The one about riding a horse to Banbury Cross."

"I could check out the stories related to Banbury Cross." Artemis suggested. "Maybe we could find the original story in the process." She yawned as she spoke.

"How about we get some sleep first." Jonathan yawned as well. "We could meet up for breakfast at the library and probably start there."

"That sounds like a date." Artemis grinned.

'A date?' He repeated in his thoughts. "So I'll see you tomorrow then?" he asked, smiling at her.

"You bet. Good night." She said as she ended the call. Jonathan closed his laptop and stretched his arms out. He then got into bed and slowly drifted off to sleep, hoping to have dreams of himself and Artemis. Dreams that, for even a brief moment, would help him forget just how much pain Alex had put him through.

****

Jonathan opened his eyes and found himself standing at the gates of the University of California-Berkeley. Exactly how he got there, he couldn't say. He began to walk around the campus, wondering exactly how he got there. There was something he did notice that was odd and somewhat satisfying; no one seemed to be looking or talking about him. It was complete anonymity. Something he had hoped for ever since he first set foot on the grounds.

He stopped as he suddenly found himself on Greek Row. He braced himself for any of the fraternities to call out to him, as they normally would. But to his surprise, they didn't. Jonathan was ecstatic. He had never thought it would actually happen. He was...a regular student.

He walked along Greek Row and noticed something odd. Either he needed glasses or that the students on Greek Row were somewhat unfamiliar. He heard songs that were considered top hits five, maybe six years ago. And unless he was imagining things, he could see a familiar Jeep parked in the Sigma Chi house's parking space.

"What's that doing there?" He asked himself. Soon, he noticed that everything was getting dark, as though it was night time. That was odd. He looked at his watch and blinked in utter surprise. It was 11:20 p.m.! He looked around and saw that some of the boys at Greek Row had returned to their respective frat houses. He then noticed someone sneaking out of the Sigma Chi house.

By the light of the streetlamps, Jonathan could visibly make out the boy's features. He couldn't believe who it was. It was Alex, only he looked different and much younger. Like how he looked when he first started going to Berkeley. 'What was I seeing?' Jonathan thought. He then saw Alex get into the Jeep and start the engine. 'Where was he headed,' he thought as he ran and climbed into the back of the Jeep. He hid while Alex drove the vehicle through Greek Row, through the university streets and out of the complex.

Jonathan could see that Alex seemed to be constantly glancing at the clock on the car, as if he were rushing to make it to some appointment. 'But in the middle of the night?' They passed several shops and made several turns around streets that weren't familiar to Jonathan. 'Where was Alex heading?' He thought as he crouched under the seat and waited until finally, the Jeep came to a stop.

He watched as Alex got out of the Jeep and walked onto what looked like a dirt path. He could see Alex approach and stop in front of a gnarled tree in the middle of.... a crossroad.

'A crossroad? What is Alex doing here?' Jonathan then saw the clock on the car. It was midnight. And at that exact moment, he heard clip clopping hooves trotting along one of the paths. He looked to the direction that Alex was looking and gasped.

Coming down the path was the Lady on the Horse!

'What in the heck?' Jonathan thought. Alex.... summoned the Lady? He watched as the Lady stopped in front of his brother and began to speak to him. "What do you ask of me?" He heard the Lady ask Alex.

"Don't say anything, Alex." Jonathan muttered in a pleading tone, realizing what Alex was going to do. "It's not worth it!"

But his pleas fell on deaf ears as Alex looked to the Lady and replied. "To leave a legacy unlike no other...." He watched as the Lady reached for one of the rings on her fingers and pulled out a familiar golden band set, with an emerald stone surrounded by four diamonds. He watched as she delicately handed the ring to Alex before uttering.

"You shall have your wish.... take heed.... for I shall come to collect..."

"ALEX, WHAT HAVE YOU DONE!?" Jonathan cried out as he leapt from the Jeep and ran towards his brother, as the Lady on the Horse rode away into the darkness. Jonathan grabbed Alex by the shoulders and looked at him. "Alex, why did you do it? Do you have any idea what's going to happen to you when she comes?"

Alex stared blankly at Jonathan; his gaze unfazed at Jonathan's question. Then he suddenly opened his mouth and replied. "Help me..."

"Help me..." Jonathan heard another voice behind him. He looked over his shoulder and saw Claire O' Hara standing behind him, her hands outstretched in a pleading manner. "Help us..."

"Help me...Jon..." Jonathan looked back towards Alex and gasped in horror as a pair of delicate, spectral hands grabbed Alex and pulled him away into the darkness. "Help me, Jon!" He cried out, stretching his hands out.

Jonathan rushed forward and grabbed Alex's hands. He tried to pull Alex back towards him, but he was stopped as the Lady on the Horse appeared behind Alex and glared at Jonathan. "He's mine." She cried in an unearthly screech, as she pulled Alex further into the darkness.

"Jon! Help me!" Alex cried.

"ALEX!" Jonathan cried out, trying desperately to reach him when he woke up sweating and breathing heavily. He quickly sat up on his bed and let out deep, erratic breaths. 'A nightmare? It was just a nightmare.' He thought as he looked around his room. "It was just a nightmare." He told himself. "But...the ring..."

'Could it be that the nightmare he had was something of a warning? That Alex had done something and if so, was his own brother in trouble? And if Alex really did summon the Lady, what could he do to save him?' Jonathan spent the rest of the night pondering on the nightmare and the questions in his mind, wondering what he ought to do next.

<u>Chapter 5</u>

"What can I get you, sugar?" the waitress asked as she held her notepad and pen, taking the orders. She watched as Jonathan read the menu from cover to cover. Artemis was sitting across Jonathan as she read her menu, occasionally looking up to look at Jonathan. She could see, even if others didn't, that Jonathan hadn't been sleeping at all.

She looked at her menu again and said. "Can we get two hot cups of coffee and some pancakes and bacon?"

The waitress nodded, her pen tip scratching against the paper's surface. "So pancakes and bacon for you as well, sugar?" she asked Jonathan. He looked up and said. "Yeah…and can we get also some waffles and eggs?" She scribbled down their orders and took the menus with her, promising their orders in 15 minutes. As soon as the waitress had gone, Artemis placed both her hands on the table and said.

"Alright, something's up. You haven't been sleeping properly. I can see it in your eyes."

Jonathan yawned for a brief moment as she spoke. "Is it that obvious?" Artemis narrowed her eyes and pursed her lips at him as if asking him 'why ask an obvious question?' He sighed and said. "I couldn't sleep well, sorry."

"I'm sure you probably were bothered by what happened between you and your brother." Artemis said, just as the waitress returned with the two cups of coffee. "I'm sure if you sat down and had a heart to heart, it will be alright. "

"It doesn't have anything to do with what happened between me and Alex." Jonathan said as he picked up the cup of coffee with slightly trembling hands. Something that Artemis was quick to notice. She reached out and held his hand as if to help him calm down. He looked at her and let out a deep breath. "I had a nightmare." He added. "Or at least, I think it was a nightmare."

"Okay, that's random." She replied. "It must have been a really bad nightmare for you to not sleep at all." The waitress had returned with their orders, and while Jonathan poured a plateful of syrup onto his pancakes and waffles, she added, "Was it that bad a nightmare?"

"I don't think it was a nightmare, Artemis." He took a deep breath and replied. "I saw Alex making a deal with the Lady on the Horse."

"What?!" Artemis asked in complete amazement. "You sure?"

"I can never forget the Lady's face, Artemis." Jonathan said.

"Well, what did your brother ask her?" She asked.

"To leave a legacy unlike any other." He replied, remembering the words as though they were fresh on his mind. "I think...I think he asked her to make him who he is now."

"You mean, all those things your brother did when he was in college that was because he asked the Lady?" Artemis asked. "Isn't that a bit..."

"Farfetched?" he finished. "You could say that. But, now that I think about it, Alex wasn't always the superstar that he is now."

"And you would know how?" Artemis asked, brandishing a fork with pancake pieces skewered on it.

Jonathan looked at her and replied. "Well, I grew up with him, for starters." He chewed on his pancakes and after taking another swig of coffee, added. "His popularity back in high school was limited to just being a football athlete and student body president. I don't remember him being an overachiever of sorts. It started when he was already at Berkeley."

"I see…" Artemis said. "What do you think he meant by, legacy?"

"I don't know." Jonathan shrugged. "But I think it's because he's a legacy too. He got into Berkeley because Dad and Grandpa were from Berkeley too." Did this mean he wanted to be a different legacy? He thought to himself. But then, he's already successful. Surely it wasn't because of the Lady on the Horse.

"Honestly, Artemis. "He began. "I'm not even sure if he made a deal with her or not. A part of me hopes that it was just a nightmare." But I can't understand why I don't feel that way.

Sensing that the mood had gotten a bit dark, Artemis decided to lighten it up. "Well, you can't figure that out on an empty stomach now, can you?" Jonathan looked up and after a few seconds, chuckled. 'She was right,' he thought. 'I can't think straight if I'm not at my best.'

"You're right." He said as he picked up his fork and ate his breakfast. "Thanks, Artemis. Lately, I have been out of sorts. This whole business with the Lady on the Horse, Claire's accident and Alex showing up…it messes you up, you know."

"I know." She replied. "Hasn't been easy on my part as well." She drank her coffee and sighed. "Claire's parents came over this morning for her things. They asked me if I knew anything about her."

"And?"

"I shook my head and told them we weren't that close." Artemis looked at her cup. "She was nice on occasion. Heck she was the one who told me I should wear girly clothes more often. I feel really bad not telling them, to be honest."

"Do you think they'll believe what you say?" He asked. Artemis shook her head. 'That was a given,' he thought. After all, any sane, rational thinking person wouldn't say that someone died because of a bargain made with an alleged supernatural being.

They finished their brunch, headed out of the diner and walked back to the university. Despite the heat of the morning sun, it was oddly cold that they didn't need umbrellas or even scarves. It was a normal day. 'Hard to believe,' Jonathan thought, that the night before was quite eventful to say the least. But in a way, it lightened the load on his person. And even if Alex would never apologize or admit his shortcomings to Jonathan, deep down, he still cared for his brother.

They approached the main building, where they saw a large group of students speaking to one another in excited voices, as they gathered by a small raised platform. There, to his surprise and subtle annoyance, Jonathan saw Alex standing next to a group of Sigma Chi boys and their president, looking both dignified and statuesque.

"Wonder what your brother's up to?" Artemis whispered as they stood under a tree, taking care not to draw near to the ground.

"Something superstar related." Jonathan said with contempt, as the Sigma Chi president hushed the excited crowd. He then cleared his throat and began to speak.

"Are you ready to meet a legend?" He roared through his microphone. The students, particularly the girls, screamed in excitement as they glanced at Alex who simply waved and smiled at them. "Well, here he is! Sigma Chi's Legendary Super Star and All

Time Quarterback of the Year, Alexander 'Alex the Stampede....

Madden!"

'Alex the Stampede,' Jonathan muttered amusedly at the epithet his brother had. Then again, he was quite good at football. Perhaps the epithet came after he got his super star status...or after the Lady granted him the wish. He was still bothered by the nightmare and couldn't tell if it was real or not. Jonathan watched as Alex stepped up to the front and greeted the excited crowd.

"Thank you everyone." He said. "I'm so happy to be back on campus. I have such fond memories of walking the very same pavement paths and sitting in the same chairs as you did...hell, even going to college parties and staying out until the crack of dawn."

There came a loud cheer from the crowd, while Jonathan scoffed at that statement. "That makes sense." He muttered. "Alex was always smelling like booze. But he always got away with it." He watched as the students cheered on as Alex went on speaking. He then jolted for a moment as Alex's gaze met with Jonathan's.

"Everyone." Alex began. "I'd like you all to meet a very special person. My little brother, Jonathan." He then directed everyone's gaze towards the tree where Jonathan and Artemis stood. Immediately, the students began to talk among themselves while they looked at Jonathan. He could hear the same phrases being uttered as they looked at him,

"Did you know he was Alex's brother?"

"Whoa, he's in my Math class..."

"He's kinda cute in a...rocker type of way."

"Yeah, they look alike..."

"How come he isn't in Sigma Chi, like his brother?"

This was what he had hoped to avoid ever since he started school. Jonathan groaned at the prospect that his hopes of finishing college as an anonymous and ordinary student, had long flown out of the window, as the boys of Sigma Chi cheered. One of the boys then noticed Artemis and cried out. "LOOK, EVERYONE! ALEX MADDEN'S BABY BROTHER EVEN HAS A BEAUTIFUL GIRLFRIEND!"

'The hell?!' Jonathan thought as he glanced at Artemis whose cheeks had turned beet red with embarrassment. He slowly frowned and grit his teeth, as several of the Sigma Chi boys escorted him past the crowd, and up the makeshift stage where he stood next to Alex in front of everyone. Alex then placed his arm around Jonathan and beamed happily towards the crowd, which gradually increased as more students and even some faculty members drew nearer to the stage.

"I am happy to invite all of you to the opening ceremony of the newly inaugurated Alexander Madden Hall this coming Friday." He said.

The crowd let out an enormous cheer and applause as one of the Sigma Chi boys added. "And his little brother and his girlfriend will be there as well." Jonathan could see from afar how red and embarrassed Artemis had grown. He quickly got down and wove his way through the crowd towards Artemis.

"Let's go." He said as he held her hand. She nodded and they briskly walked away from the crowd; with the Sigma Chi boys crying out.

"Aww the lovebirds are gone folks. Best give the younger Madden space to ask her personally!" which was then followed by another round of enormous cheers and applauses.

Jonathan and Artemis walked as fast as they could, evading several students who were now staring at them completely. He had never felt more awkward and embarrassed in his life. And as much as he wouldn't mind all the embarrassment he would encounter; it was Artemis he was worried about. How could Alex let the Sigma Chi boys do that? Worse, how could he just stand there and do nothing?

"Jonathan, stop. Wait." Artemis said as she stopped in her tracks and let out deep breaths.

"I'm sorry." Jonathan quickly said. "I'm really sorry. About...about earlier." He looked at her with an apologetic expression. "I didn't think they would..."

"It's no big deal, Jonathan." She said. "Maybe it was all for laughs or something."

"How can you not be embarrassed?" he asked. "My brother just placed us in an awkward situation back there! I swear, Alex..."

"There you are!" Jonathan turned around and glared as Alex walked towards them happily. "I was wondering where you both ran off to." He started. "Listen, about earlier..."

BAM!

Like a scene from any movie that involved punching, Jonathan mustered up whatever strength he had in his fiber and punched his older brother square in the face, sending Alex Madden falling to the ground. At that exact moment, several students had gathered nearby upon hearing the sound of Alex's Madden voice.

Alex looked at his brother as he massaged his jaw while Jonathan let out erratic breaths. "WHAT THE HELL HAS GOTTEN

INTO YOU, JON!?" Alex cried out as he got up and patted himself down.

"You got a lot of nerve asking me that!" Jonathan said, his anger swelling up. "What the hell was that back there? Putting me and Artemis in your little show!?"

"Look, it was just for laughs." Alex said. "I tried telling the boys not to say anything that would embarrass you"

"Gee, you really tried?" Jonathan asked sarcastically. "Didn't look like that to me." He folded his arms and frowned at Alex.

"Look, I'm sorry about that." He said. "But you didn't have to slug me, you know. Where the hell did you get all that strength?"

"I've been meaning to punch you ever since day one." Jonathan barked. "And here I was contemplating on talking to you about last night. But I guess my brother's college legacy is more important than patching things up with family."

"You know, we can talk about that, if you'll just let me-"

"Let you what, Alex?" Jonathan asked. "Let you explain? What's there to explain?" And he began to speak in a rather high pitched and sarcastic tone. "You didn't do anything wrong. Your little brother is just being moody. You have nothing to worry about."

He sighed and added. "Look, I have to go to class. So if you want to talk, we can talk maybe after your big day." And he turned on his heel and both he and Artemis walked away, once again ignoring the stares from the rest of the students. He was not in the mood at all, and while he still had an ounce of respect for his brother, he decided not to engage any further.

Alex had gone to the men's room and splashed some cold water on his face, gently patting the part where Jonathan had punched him. He had never expected his own brother to punch, let alone have the strength to do that. He had always known his brother to be the gentler and more reserved of the both of them. As the water trickled down his cheeks to the sink, Alex could still vividly hear Jonathan's angry words echo in his mind.

"...my brother's college legacy is more important than patching things up with family..."

"That's not true." Alex said to his reflection in the mirror. "Not true at all." He stared at himself before glancing at the ring on his finger. He tried to shrug it off and kept telling himself that he was never at all concerned with his legacy.

But if there was one thing that not even Alex Madden knew, it was that he was more excited than anyone else about his upcoming event. It's not every day you get a call from the university president, telling you that the newly constructed building would be named in honor of the prestige you brought to the college. And that was what was going on through Alex's mind, among other things.

Ever since he graduated from Berkeley, it seemed that multi-million-dollar deals and opportunities had come knocking at his door in the form of talent scouts and head hunters, looking to recruit the famous college football star as a rookie for their respective football teams. Businessmen offering him managerial positions. Fellowships to several exclusive clubs, and even honorary degrees in different schools.

To say that he reveled in this was a slight understatement on his part. Alex was the type of man who, for the most part, tried his best to put on an air of humility when people praised his achievements. And when people asked him what his secret was, he would merely say.

"Hard work and determination and proper time management."

Tried and tested method, yes. But an overly used response. In truth, things came easy for Alex, and only he knew the real reason why. He washed his face once more and grabbed a piece of tissue paper to wipe it dry while staring at the mirror.

'Hard to believe I looked different a few years ago,' he told himself, fondly remembering his younger days when he first started at Berkeley. The door opened and Alex heard a familiar voice speak to him. "Well, well...Alex Madden. Didn't think I'd be seeing you back on campus so soon."

Alex turned around to see a tall, muscular man dressed in a pair of black jogging pants, a collared t-shirt bearing the university's seal, and a cap showing the college's football team mascot. On the man's muscular arms were several tattoos. Alex smiled and said. "Hello, Grover. Long-time no see."

"Hey, boy. How you been?" Grover Johnson said, extending his hand out to shake Alex's.

Alex shook his hand and stared at him from head to toe. It had been a long time since he last saw Grover. They had both tried out for the football team at the same time and were teammates during their college years. And now, judging by Grover's attire and his faculty ID, Alex deduced that Grover was now the college football coach.

"Doing alright." Alex replied. "I see you're the new football coach."

"Yeah, I took over Coach Jones job two years ago after he decided to move to Australia." Grover said.

"And how's the team since then?" Alex asked.

Grover scratched his head as he washed his hands by the sink. "They're okay." He replied. "Not as organized as us back in the day, but I sure as hell will drill their silly asses into shape."

"We weren't that organized, Grover." Alex said, managing a little chuckle. "In fact, if I recall, we didn't like working together." He began to remember the times when he and Grover would often argue about strategies at first, before eventually warming up to one another.

"Yeah..." Grover said. "I mean, you were some overly confident white guy and I didn't like that it came so easy for you."

"You're seriously pulling the race card, huh?" Alex said.

"Yeah, but that was before, fool!" They walked past several cabinets that showcased various trophies and photos of past football teams; some which Alex would recognize as members of his own team. He would even see a young Grover and Eric Douglas standing with a much younger Alex Madden, as they smiled and held the championship cup. Alex stared at the photos and thought of those wonderful times. Grover drew near and looked at the same photos.

"I remember that game." He said, pointing to one photo. "That was the game they dubbed 'The Miracle from the Heavens.' Remember that?"

"I remember." Alex said. "It was in the last quarter and we had to score only 2 points to win the game. We only had 30 seconds to the clock."

"That was the game where you held the ball and you charged through all the players until you made the crucial touchdown and won the game." Grover said. "That was when you earned the nickname, The Stampede."

"It feels corny now that I think about it." He said, chuckling at the name. "But to be honest, I was running on adrenaline then."

"Well, whatever you were on then, it helped us win the season!" Grover said, patting Alex on the back. Alex chuckled as he stared at the photo. He then had a thought and looked at Grover.

"Hey, mind if I asked you something?" he began.

Grover looked at him and said. "Sure, brother. What's on your mind?"

"Do you remember that urban legend game that was going around on campus back then?" Alex asked. "The one about going to a crossroad at night?"

"You mean the one about some fancy white lady on a horseback who grants wishes and favors?" Grover finished, looking at Alex. When he nodded, Grover chuckled and leaned against the wall next to the display cabinets. "Why do you ask?"

"Just thought about it." Alex said. "Were you ever tempted to try it?"

"Seriously?" He asked. "It was too creepy. Even for me. The girls over at Sorority row said they wanted to try it, but they were too scared to do it."

"Did you...believe it was real then?" Alex asked.

Grover shook his head. "Nah, I thought it was one of those urban legend stories nerds talk about." Then he added. "Strangely though, people are talking about the story all over again. And I heard your brother was a witness to some girl's accident."

"So I've heard." He replied. "He won't tell me anything." Not even if I ask him nicely, he thought to himself. He wondered still why Jonathan was somewhat hostile and aggressive towards him.

"Yeah, your little brother seems to be...an oddball, isn't he? "Grover said. "Won't even try out for the football team? Shame really. He has a good body build." 'Sports was never Jonathan's thing.' Alex thought. "So why the sudden interest in that Lady story?"

"How did it go again?" The two men had exited the main building and were now walking towards the football field, where Alex could hear the sound of voices calling out familiar words and phrases used in football. Grover replied. "Well, if I remember the story, if you go to a crossroad where four paths pan out at midnight, a beautiful woman dressed in white silk, with gold rings and gold bells will appear on horseback. She will ask you your deepest wish, and if she gives you a ring, that means the wish will be granted."

"But when that wish is fulfilled, the Lady will appear once more and ask for the ring back as well as.... your price."

"What price was that?" Alex asked.

Grover shrugged. "I don't know. But most of the time, they say that the price is something that is never spoken, but is very important."

"Didn't they also mention there was...a way for the Lady to not collect that unknown price?" Alex asked.

"They did, but I don't know what it is." Grover said. "Hey, let's not talk about that. The boys will be so happy to finally meet The Stampede."

He then led Alex towards the football field where a group of boys were running laps on the field. Immediately, memories of his days doing exactly the same thing they were doing flooded into his mind. He could remember sweating profusely, but getting into the football team was just one of the many wishes the Lady had granted him.

And yet, Alex wondered about that unknown price the Lady would come to collect? And if he could avoid giving her that price. While Grover was introducing him to the football team, Alex could hear an odd and faint sound in the distance. If he didn't know any better, it sounded like...twinkling bells.

****

"Did you really punch Alex 'The Stampede' Madden?" Dick asked in utter disbelief and horror. Jonathan stared at his roommate and strangely, his neighbor Milo, as they sat on the bunkbeds and eyed him down. He had not expected to be 'ambushed' by these two inside his room.

"Dude, did you really punch Alex Madden?!" Dick repeated the question once more.

Jonathan groaned and said. "Why do you want to know?"

"Don't change the subject, Jonny boy!" Dick said as he leaned in closer to Jonathan from the edge of the bed. "Did you punch him?"

"And what if I did?" Jonathan began. "It's none of your concern."

Dick let out what one would describe as an agonized cry, while Milo stared at Jonathan in awe and silence. Jonathan knew that Dick idolized his brother and he could probably assume what Dick would say. His assumptions were proven true when Dick let out a deep breath and exclaimed.

"HOLY SHIT! YOU ACTUALLY PUNCHED THE STAMPEDE?"

"His name is Alex." Jonathan groaned. "And again, why is that so important? He's my brother and we had...issues."

"I still cannot believe you would harm your older brother, mon ami." Milo said. "I did not zake you for a, how do you say it, a 'personne violente'."

"I'm not really a violent person, if that's what you're saying, Milo." Jonathan said. "But there were some things that needed to be addressed and let's say it's been a long time coming..." Jonathan was the non-confrontational kind of guy. But, as he said, there were certain things that couldn't be suppressed any longer. That, and coupled with the constant visions of the Lady on the Horse, would make someone like Jonathan snap, even for a brief moment.

"Well, eef zat iz ze case, mon ami..." Milo said. "I still zay zat you and your brother should talk about ze issues you are 'aving."

"It's easier said than done, Milo." Jonathan said. "Now, if it's alright with you Dick, I wanted to talk with Milo alone."

"Yeah, man. Whatever." Dick said as he slung his backpack on his shoulder and headed to the door. "I'm gonna be late for my bio exam, anyhow."

"Now that's a first." Jonathan said. "I don't remember seeing you take your studies seriously..."

"If I don't get a grade above C in this exam, I might as well kiss that hot girl goodbye." Dick said as he closed the door behind him, leaving Jonathan and Milo all alone in the room.

Jonathan gestured for Milo to sit in Dick's rarely used desk. As Milo sat down, Jonathan opened his laptop and looked at him.

"There's something I want to ask you." He began. "But you gotta swear that you won't think I'm insane or nuts. Alright?"

"Ah mon ami, you 'ave my word." Milo said reassuring him.

"Alright." Jonathan let out a deep breath and said. "Do you remember me asking you about Faustian contracts?"

"Ah, but of course." Milo replied. "You were curious about ze whole concept of deals with ze devil. Why ask about zat once more?"

"You have heard the rumors about me and Artemis being present at the time that girl, Claire was killed, right?" When Milo nodded, Jonathan continued. "Artemis and I think Claire asked the Lady on the Horse to make her famous. And when she got what she wanted, the Lady came for her and took her soul."

A rational thinking person would think a story like that would be too fantastical to believe. A rational thinking person would say that there had to be a logical explanation. A rational thinking person would even say that the person telling him this claim must be mad and insane. But Milo was a different person. From the moment they first met to the time they shared coffee in his room, Jonathan could tell that Milo Garnier was not one who would judge a person so quickly.

"Do you 'ave at least proof of zis claim, mon ami?" he asked.

"Well, on the night she was killed, Artemis and I saw her spirit standing next to her body." Jonathan replied. "Right before she was taken away by the Lady on the Horse, she called out to us and said. 'Help me....'"

"You saw 'er spirit being taken away by ze Dame à cheval?" Milo repeated, looking at Jonathan before crossing himself. "Sacre' bleu. Zat is indeed a terrifying thought, no?"

"I know you're probably thinking I'm starting to sound crazy, but ever since that day...me and Artemis have been having...visions about the Lady on the Horse." Jonathan continued. "And quite recently, I had this dream where I saw" And here he hesitated for a moment, wondering what it would garner from him if he spoke it.

"You saw what, mon ami?"

He let out a deep sigh and replied. "I saw my brother Alex going to a crossroad at night and he made a deal with her. That would explain why my brother is what he is."

There was silence after he spoke. Jonathan waited for Milo's reaction and wondered whether Milo would think him insane or believe him. Milo settled back in the chair and seemed to be in deep thought. Then he pursed his lips together and said.

"You know, mon ami. I was reading zat story in ze internet. Zere is apparently a way to avoid paying ze unknown price."

'A way?' Jonathan had not heard about this? So did this mean that there was a way to avoid having the unnamed price paid? Milo then continued his story. "Oui, zer is a way to protect yourself from ze Lady, but it is not zo good either."

"What is it?" He asked.

Milo looked at Jonathan and replied. "To avoid paying ze unnamed price, you must pass ze Lady's token to anuzzer."

Jonathan was horrified at that notion. Pass the ring to someone else? Did that mean the Lady would take that person in their place? He got up from his seat and exclaimed. "No way! There is no way in hell that they should do that." How could anyone even think of that as a solution to avoiding the Lady's due?

"Zat is why ze game must never be played." Milo said. "It is ze Devil's game. I do not mean zo condemn, mon ami. But anyone who plays zat game is damned."

At that exact moment, there came a knock on Jonathan's door. He got up and opened it to see one of the boys from the dorm. "Hey Madden, y-y-y-you got a visitor." He said. Jonathan noticed that the boy was stammering as though he just met someone really famous...

"A visitor?" he asked. "Who?" The boy stammered and replied. "Y-y-your girlfriend. She's waiting in the lounge. I-I didn't know you had a girlfriend."

'Girlfriend? Artemis!?' He then walked past the boy and down the stairs to see Artemis sitting on the couch in the lounge, a look of worry crossed over her face. "Artemis, what's wrong?" Jonathan asked as he sat on the couch next to her.

"I saw her." She said. "I saw the Lady on campus!"

****

Alex watched as Grover introduced the football team members to the legendary Alex 'The Stampede' Madden. He could see their excited faces as they began to ask him various questions about his time in college, the many football games he had won and even the 'legendary' things he had done with the Sigma Chi fraternity.

"How did you get the nickname 'The Stampede'?" One boy asked.

"You idiot, he said it was during the "Miracle from the Heavens game." Another boy said.

"Oh, sorry about that." The first boy said. "It's just that, you're so cool and they said you were the youngest quarterback in the history of the university."

Grover then blew the whistle around his neck, signaling the football team to assemble in front of him. In an instant, the boys gathered around and stood at attention, as Alex walked to the benches and sat down to watch them. Grover then instructed the boys to review various game strategies and maneuvers.

While the team went on with their drills, Alex watched and recalled the days when he played football. He had not realized that the field had slowly begun to grow dark. After a few minutes, he got up and walked to the coach's office to get a glass of water. The office was located across the football field. 'No worries,' he thought to himself, as he excused himself and walked across the football field.

As he crossed the field, he noticed the sky had begun to grow grey and cloudy. 'Was it going to rain?' He thought. Then, he saw mist slowly appear and envelope the entire field. Alex kept on walking, trying his best to get across the field. But it felt like he was walking for what seemed like forever, unsure of where he was headed or if he was near his destination.

He then noticed a figure standing in the distance. 'Was it Grover?' Alex walked towards the figure, feeling a sudden drop in the temperature. He began to let out breaths that were so cold that he could even see them escape from his lips. 'What was happening right now?' He stopped for a moment as he stared at the figure.

He blinked for a moment and rubbed his eyes once more. If he didn't know any better, it looked like the figure was walking towards him! He stood there, practically frozen in his tracks as the figure began to approach him. He then heard the sound of twinkling bells and the gentle neigh of a horse, and he knew right there and then who was approaching him. Slowly, but surely, the delicate and ethereal figure of the Lady appeared before Alex.

"Alex Madden..." He heard her speak from beneath the veil. "The ring..."

Alex glanced at his hand where the ring was. He could see the ruby stone was as bright and red as blood; something he had never seen before. He looked at the Lady and then said. "Why have you come?"

"On the fifth day..." he heard her say. "The legacy shall be made and the debt will be paid."

"Legacy? Fifth day?" he repeated. "I...I can't. Not yet. I...I'm not ready."

"Perhaps, you would rather have someone else pay the debt?" she asked. "Your.... brother, perhaps?"

"No, you leave Jonathan out of this." He said. "He has no idea about this at all. I..." Alex was somewhat at a loss of words. He would never consider that option.

The Lady walked closer to him, raised her delicate hands to his cheeks and gently stroked them. "On the fifth day of the seven days then..." She then walked back into the mist and shadows, leaving Alex to stare blankly as the mist slowly disappeared.

He soon found himself standing at the edge of the field, next to the doors that led to the coach's office. In the distance, he saw Grover and the football team doing their drills and exercises. Alex then made his way out of the field and into the building, slowly contemplating on what he had just felt and heard.

'The fifth day of the seven days. That's what the Lady said.' he thought. It then dawned on him what she meant and he began to realize that he may not have enough time left.

There was one thing he had to do; he needed to speak to Jonathan before Friday's event; before his legacy would be named; before it was too late...

<u>Chapter 6</u>

Artemis was worried. Right after Jonathan punched Alex, the two of them left Alex standing in the hallway. She could tell that punching his older brother took out a lot on Jonathan's psyche. They both stopped in front of the main building, where Jonathan had punched the wall once more and cried out in anger.

"Dammit!" He shook his reddening hand. "Dammit all." He started punching the wall over and over again, not caring at all if it was already hurting or swelling.

"Jonathan, calm down!" Artemis cried out as she seized his hands and stopped him. "You can't do this to yourself."

"I just can't believe that guy!" He exclaimed. "What the hell was he even thinking? Everything is just an opportunity for him."

"You need to calm down, Jonathan." She said. "Getting mad won't solve anything."

"Wouldn't you be upset too if someone put you through a seriously awkward and embarrassing situation?" He asked. "Wouldn't you be mad?"

"I would. But that doesn't mean I should lose my shit." She replied. "You need to keep a calm head. Now, breathe in...and out." She began to breathe in and out herself.

Jonathan sighed and began to take in deep breaths. After a few minutes or so, his anger somehow managed to die down as he leaned against the back rest of the stone benches. He rested his head on the back and Artemis followed as well, resting her head on the back of the bench. They both stared at the clear sky and took in the smell of the clean air, and the sound of leaves rustling against the grass.

"Why is it so hard to not hate him?" Jonathan asked.

"Simple…. he is your brother." Artemis said.

"Sometimes, I wish he weren't so famous." He said. "I wish he was just a regular guy like everyone else."

"Better be careful when you wish for something, Jonathan." She said. "You never know if you'll end up wishing to her." She chuckled at her own joke. Jonathan looked at her and chuckled as well. They continued to stare at the sky for some time, before Jonathan finally exhaled and stretched his arms out. He looked over at Artemis, and once again his heart began to beat, as their close proximity forged in him an intense need to tell her how he felt.

But before he could say anything, Artemis then said. "You know, all you have to do is have a heart to heart with your brother. Everything will be better once you do."

"Maybe when I've cooled down." He said.

"Well, I suggest you do it before it's too late." She said getting up. "Anyway, I need to get to class. Will you be alright?"

"Yeah." Jonathan replied as he got up as well. "I'll be ok. Thanks, Artemis."

"Anytime." She said, before waving good-bye and walking away from Jonathan.

As she walked along the cobbled stone path towards the main building, Artemis touched her chest and still felt her heart beat quite fast. She didn't realize it then, but lately, she had been feeling her heart beat as though it were excited to have been close to Jonathan.

She had never been this close to anyone before, and when she first came to Berkeley, she had expected to just get through college without getting close to anyone. But after meeting Jonathan, it seemed that her plans were taking a more interesting direction.

She had never experienced having a close male friend. Or even considered the idea of dating a boy. But Jonathan was different. She felt very secure and comfortable with him that it was almost a pain not to be near him. She felt happy whenever they would talk, be it on video calls or instant messaging. She enjoyed having coffee or brunch whenever he invited her to it, and more importantly, with the recent event that had somewhat involved the both of them, she felt more at ease in having someone to lean on to.

Ever since witnessing Claire's unfortunate death and seeing visions of a spectral Lady, Artemis knew all too well that what she and Jonathan were experiencing would normally make any rational thinking person question reality. She knew how tough it was to keep their emotions in check; especially if it would make them break down in utter despair. She could imagine just how emotionally upset Jonathan could possibly be, with the sudden appearance of his older brother; what suppressed emotions he had when he found out the truth about his college admission...

"He must really be having a hard time." She thought to herself. She wanted very much to help him, but she knew that this was something he had to deal with on his own.

She sighed and had started to walk past the football field, when she saw Alex walking across the field towards an adjacent building. She wondered if she could possibly talk to him and probably convince him to listen to Jonathan. She had slowly begun making her way towards him, when she suddenly noticed a strange fog appear out of nowhere and cover the entire football field.

Artemis was now walking blindly, all the while wondering where it came from. She suddenly saw a tall figure appear in the distance. To her surprise, the figure seemed to be moving towards what looked like another figure. She squinted her eyes for a bit, hoping to catch a glimpse of the shape. But the fog was so thick that she couldn't see what it was.

Then, she saw the shape slowly move away. At the same time, the fog began to lift slowly, giving Artemis a chance to see clearly. She gasped at the sight. Even through the lifting fog, she could see the figure's features as clear as day.

It was the Lady on the Horse!

Artemis's jaw was completely frozen in horror. There was hardly any sound that came out of her, as she saw the veiled Lady astride on a huge white horse. Slowly, she stepped back and watched as the Lady rode away into the fading fog and disappeared completely. Artemis blinked and rubbed her eyes. She immediately looked at the football field and saw Alex staring in the direction where the Lady had disappeared to.

'It can't be...' she thought as she turned on her heel and ran as fast as she could. "Class can wait." She told herself as she ran. "I have to tell Jonathan..."

****

There is a reason why there are more than 30 dormitories on campus. There were at least 3000 students attending Berkeley each year, and at least 60% of these students had come from different states or countries. The dormitories were equally divided for both men and women, and as such, there were a couple of rules to abide by. One such rule stated that as much as possible, the two sexes must be separated at all costs.

After all, men and women did things differently in their respective dorms. And it was a rare occasion that girls would visit boys in their dormitories. Then again, Artemis was not like most girls. She sat patiently and waited for Jonathan to come down. She gripped the strap of her bag as she nervously waited, all the while avoiding the stares the boys were giving her.

When Jonathan appeared, she immediately got up and began to speak. "Jonathan...there you are...I...I..."

"Artemis, what's wrong?" he asked as he sat down next to her. He could see the worry on her face, the kind one would have if they had seen a ghost.

Artemis looked at him and said. "I saw her...I saw the Lady."

Jonathan looked over his shoulder and noticed several boys were staring at the both of them. He then leaned in and whispered. "Do you want to talk in a more private place?"

Artemis saw the boys and she quickly nodded. Jonathan walked back up to his room and grabbed his backpack. He hurried back down and soon they left the boys dormitory, headed towards some of the stone benches that were scattered around campus. Once they sat down, Jonathan looked at Artemis and then said.

"Okay, we're alone now. Now start from the beginning. What do you mean, you saw the lady?"

Artemis let out deep breaths and replied. "Well, I'm not really sure anymore. But I was heading to main building for class, and I was passing by the football field where I saw your brother, Alex."

"Okay..." He said. "And then?"

"I wanted to talk to him about a couple of things. Mostly you, actually." She said. "But that's beside the point. So I started to walk towards him when all of a sudden, a strange fog appeared and the entire field was completely covered in it. I couldn't see where I was going, nor could I see anything at all."

'A strange and unexpected fog?' Jonathan repeated. Artemis then continued. "Then I saw a large shape appear out of nowhere. I couldn't see what it was at first, but I then I saw it leave and when the fog started to disintegrate, I saw what the shape was. Or rather, who it was. I saw the Lady."

"She appeared in the football field?" Jonathan asked. Why would she appear in the football field? "Did someone summon her?"

"No, Jonathan." Artemis said. "Remember the story? She can only come when you go to a crossroad. So, she probably came for somebody. Or...visited someone."

"Why do you say that?"

"Because when she rode away, the fog disappeared and I saw your brother staring at the direction to where she disappeared." Artemis said.

Alex was staring after the Lady? Jonathan lowered his head and began to ponder and worry. If what Artemis said was true, then it only confirmed his worst nightmare. Alex must have summoned the Lady before. And now she had come to haunt him and most likely...collect. "Jonathan..." Artemis began. "You have got to ask your brother if he really did call on the Lady."

'If he really did ask the Lady for a wish, then he knew too well what he was getting himself into.' He thought. At that moment, he suddenly grew angrier than ever before. All those great things he had heard from his brother; all the stories and comparisons he was told of by other people; all of the achievements his brother had...they were never earned by hard work. He had to resort...to an easier method. And that made Jonathan Madden even more furious.

"If he called on the Lady, then good!" he said through gritted teeth.

"Jonathan!" Artemis said. "What do you mean by that?"

"I mean what I'm saying." He said. "Alex made a deal with her, and if she's coming to collect whatever unnamed price is demanded, then good for him."

"You can't possibly mean that, Jonathan." She said. "We have to ask him if he really did ask her. Then if he did, we have to help him."

"There's no point in helping him." He said. "You don't know what it's like. To always have to put up with everybody constantly comparing you to someone who they say is the epitome of hard work and success; to always tell yourself that you don't need to hear the obvious."

There was an immense pain in his voice as he spoke. A pain that Artemis was quick to notice. The kind that was the result of months, maybe even years of suppressing his emotions.

"All my life, I looked up to Alex because even if he was constantly being praised, he never once rubbed it in my face. He always told me that I could be my own person, and that he would support my decision. And then when I found out that he had a hand in my admission being accepted, what do you think that says about his faith in me? He didn't think I could do it at all. And now the possibility that all of Alex's success came from a wish he made to some supernatural Lady, what do you think that says about him? That his life, the life and success I admired, was all a lie!"

"Jonathan, I get it." She said in a soothing voice. "It sucks yes. What Alex did to you was a betrayal of the trust you had in him. But he is still your brother. And regardless of what he has done, he needs your help."

"If he needed my help, he would just have to say so." Jonathan said, putting his foot down and folding his arms. Truth be told, what he was feeling validated his emotional response. What would one truly feel when someone you admired and cared for, betrayed the trust you placed on them? Regardless if they were your friend or your brother? To Jonathan, it was like someone had taken a pair of scissors and begun snipping off every possible strand of respect inside him.

And yet, there was still, even by a millimeter or so, a single strand left. He knew that despite all that he felt, Artemis was right. Alex was still his brother and he had to do something. But they were operating on an assumption, and the fact that the two of them had been having unusual moments when the Lady would appear, didn't help with the possible conclusion that Alex was in trouble.

He let out a deep sigh and said. "You're right, Artemis. He is my brother. But we don't know if he really did call on the Lady."

"Maybe you should try asking him if he did." She said.

Before Jonathan could speak, his phone started to ring. Jonathan reached into his bag and pulled out the phone. "Hello?"

He could hear the familiar accent of Milo speaking on the other end. "Jonathan, mon ami. I 'ave somezing important to tell you. It is about ze Lady Story. I zink I have found somezing zat can help."

"What?!" Jonathan replied. "Okay, where are you?"

"Meet me at ze library." Milo responded before hanging up. Jonathan quickly kept his phone and then looked at Artemis.

"Think you can cut class for today?" he asked.

"Well, technically I am." She replied. "Why?"

He went on to tell her about Milo Garnier, and how he had told him about their uncanny encounters with the Lady. "Milo's a literature major, and he sort of gave me an idea when I was doing research on the Lady. He said he might have found something about her."

"And he found it in the library?" she asked, raising an eyebrow. He nodded. She looked at her watch and said. "Well, I don't have anything planned so..."

"Alright." He said. "Let's head on over to the library. After all, we could use a little help, wouldn't you say?"

The entire campus was abuzz with the news that had begun to circulate all over. A new hall had been erected, and in a break from the tradition of naming it after Presidents, politicians or former professors, it was going to be named after a recent celebrity.

The Alexander Madden Hall. It would boast of a record breaking 40 rooms, a 150-person capacity mess hall, three common rooms, and a spacious lawn for outdoor activities and parties. It was a modern marvel to behold, and for some, a testament to the prowess and success of one of the University's finest alumnae.

The inaugural ceremony was going to be held on Friday the 13th, an inside joke by some of the board of trustees. "Madden was the pot of gold and he has always brought luck." One would say. "What better way to honor him than on a day where bad luck loses to good luck."

But Friday was something that Alex dreaded for the first time in his life. He couldn't say why, not even if people asked him if he was excited or not. For him, Friday meant the end of things. And there were things he had to do…. people he had to talk to.

"Hey, Madden." Alex looked up to see Eric and Grover walking over towards him. They stared in awe at the new hall. Grover looked at the size of it and whistled.

"Damn, that is one big hall." He said. "I heard it's going to housing foreign exchange students."

"With 40 rooms, that's gonna be a lot." Eric said. "But to have it named after you, man your family must be pretty proud of you."

"Not all are." Alex said sadly.

"Is this about the weird kid, your little brother?" Grover asked. "Man, I heard about how he sucker punched you. Didn't know the little nerd had it in him."

"Yeah, who would have thought he had it in him." Eric said. Alex then looked at the both of them with a rather irate look on his face. The two classmates looked at each other and just kept silent. They watched as the university custodians began to set the chairs and tables all over the new lawn.

It really was a sight to behold. And yet, it did not excite Alex at all. He needed to find his brother and tell him. He needed one chance. He was about to walk away when Eric said. "Hey let's check out the hall. We can get in first, right?"

"Not until the ribbon has been cut, I'm afraid. "Alex said, quickly putting on a more cordial tone. "But we can look around the grounds and perhaps...talk about Coach Jones."

"Man, do I miss the guy." Eric said as they began to walk towards the grounds. "Remember when we were so mad at him, we snuck into his office after practice and placed mousetraps all over his floor and chair."

"Yeah, we watched him sit on those mouse traps and...boom! they started snapping all over." Grover added as he started to laugh. Alex too let out a little laugh or two. It was nice to reminisce on good things, even if it were for a brief moment or two.

As they walked around the grounds, Alex looked at the ring on his finger. He knew what it meant and as the hours ticked away to the day, he then realized the truth behind the Lady's cryptic message.

On the fifth day of the seven days…. the fifth day of the week. Alex had until Friday before the Lady came for the unnamed due.

****

Jonathan and Artemis met up with Milo inside the university's library. After introducing Artemis to Milo, they immediately followed him to a section of the library, where large books were placed on top of a table near some bookcases. Jonathan glanced at the opened books on the table. He would see that some of them were written in foreign languages.

"Wow, Milo." He commented. "Even I can't read this many."

"Well, mon ami." Milo said. "I was very much intrigued by your stories about ze Lady. So I 'oped to find some truth to the story."

"Jonathan tells me you are a literature major." Artemis said. "I can't help but admire your initiative in reading more about her."

"Ah, merci, Mademoiselle Artemis." Milo said. Jonathan then opened one of the books that Milo had bookmarked. The book's pages showed various texts and illustrations that, by Milo's explanation, were dated back from the early medieval times to the early 19th century

In one of the books, Jonathan noticed a woodcut illustration of what looked like a woman dressed in fine clothes, riding a white horse. In her hand she held what looked like a riding crop, and on her toes were bells tied on a string. "Is this…her?"

Milo looked at the book and replied. "One of many variants, mon ami."

"Many variants?" Artemis asked.

"Oui." He replied. "You see, I zought about ze famous nursery rhyme and zen I decided to do a little reading. To my surprise, zis is what I 'ave found." They began to look at the books and sure enough, each of the books showed a varied illustration of the same, finely dressed woman on a horse. They were surprised to see that the story seemed to transcend both era and country.

"So how will we know where the story came from?" Artemis asked.

"Why, in ze nursery rhyme, Mademoiselle." Milo said. "'ow did it go again? Ride a cock horse....to Banbury Cross. To see a fine lady upon a white horse..."

"I don't follow." She said.

Jonathan then guessed it. "Banbury Cross. It's a town somewhere in the United Kingdom."

"How do you know there's a place like that?" Artemis asked.

"Easy...my family originated from Banbury." He replied. "The Maddens were merchants from Wales who settled in Banbury. The Banbury Cross is basically a market cross."

"Market cross?" She repeated.

"Yeah, it's like a designated marker for a market square." Jonathan said. "It often held regular markets or fairs, provided the right was granted by the monarch of the time, a bishop or a baron." Then turning to Milo, he asked. "But, what does that have to do with the Lady?"

"Ah, you asked ze right question, mon ami." Milo replied. "Truth be told, I wondered why ze rhyme specifically named Banbury Cross. And zen zat is when I found zis story."

He opened a large book and showed them a rather interesting story. Jonathan and Artemis looked at the book and saw a chapter title: THE LADY OF BANBURY. "The Lady of Banbury..." Jonathan read out loud. Artemis looked at him while Milo urged him to read. Jonathan then took the bookmark out and began to read it.

"This is interesting." He said. "According to this text, there was a young noblewoman who was married to a baron in Banbury. She was the daughter of a very wealthy merchant, who was known for her beauty and her delicate nature. But she was also known for her patronage of various artists and merchants. She would ride to the market square on a white horse and would often choose an artist or a merchant for the day, and provide them with gold coins. As a sign of gratitude, they would give her a ring. That is why her fingers had several rings on them. Sometimes, they would gift her with small bells that she would sew to her shoes and clothes."

'So that explains the whole concept of her wearing rings on her fingers and bells on her toes.' He thought to himself. But where did the whole supernatural aspect come from? He read the text once more.

"But the Lady had a secret. A terrible secret. It was said that the Lady had many lovers; most of who came from the merchants and artists she patronized. When her lord husband knew of her infidelity, he had her lovers arrested and executed. And she was confined to her rooms at the manor."

He stopped for a moment as he noticed that the story ended there. "So what happens next?" Artemis asked. Jonathan turned the pages, hoping for a continuation of sorts. "Well?"

"That's it." He said. "The story ended there."

"That's it?" She said. "But, there must be more…"

"Ah, if only, Mademoiselle." Milo sighed sadly. "Zat is all I could find. But zis is a good lead, n'est-ce pas?"

"It is." Jonathan said. "At least, there is some origin to this rhyme. And possibly the game."

"I am so sorry, mon ami if zis is all I can find for you." Milo said sadly. "Truth be told, I was 'oping to 'ave somezing zat can help you."

"It's alright." Artemis said. "This really helps a whole lot." Then she turned to face Jonathan and asked. "So what now?"

Before anyone could answer, the librarian approached them and told them it was almost time for the library to close. The three of them also checked their watches and noticed that it was nearly time for their curfew. So they got up and left the library. Milo waved them good bye with the promise that he would help them in their search.

"Do you think it was a wise idea to involve your friend, Jonathan?" Artemis asked as they began to walk side by side back to the main campus. "He doesn't think we're crazy?"

"He was the one who gave me an idea on the concept of deals with the devil." Jonathan replied. "And I think I can trust him." They walked past several groups of students and they overheard a few phrases.

"Tomorrow's the inaugural ceremony of the Madden Hall, right?"

"Yeah. Alex Madden is gonna be there!"

"I wonder if we can meet him..."

Artemis noticed Jonathan's unfazed face as they passed by the students. She wondered if he had somehow calmed down and decided not to think about it. "Will you go to the ceremony, Jonathan?" she asked

"Well, he is still my brother, as you say." He said. "And besides. He said that we would be at his ceremony. So let's not make him out as a liar..."

They reached the girls' dormitory and Jonathan escorted her to the front door. "So, I'll see you tomorrow?" He asked. She nodded and leaned forward and kissed his cheek.

"Sure." She replied. "Do me a favor and try to talk to your brother. Alright?"

"I'll try." He said, petting his cheek and giving her a smile.

****

Jonathan arrived at the dormitory and walked upstairs to his room. 'It was empty.' He thought. That meant, Dick must be out doing God knows what. He threw his backpack on the bed and sat on it. He reached for his binder and began to do his homework, as he popped his headphones on and played a song from his playlist.

'Write an essay on the importance of cultural respect.' He opened his books and turned on the light of his bedside lamp. He glanced at his books while writing down important words and phrases to be used in his essay, all the while listening to his songs play.

It took his mind off a few unpleasantries to say the least, and while he was doing his homework, he thought about his brother and what Artemis had said. A part of him did not want to go to the ceremony and the ribbon cutting. A part of him just wanted to go on without getting involved with his brother. And yet, he couldn't. Alex was still his brother and regardless of what had been said and done, Jonathan had to be the better man.

Just then, his phone rang. He picked it up and looked at the screen. It was Alex. 'Should I answer this?' He asked himself? He let out a deep sigh, pulled his headphones off and answered the phone. "Hello…"

"Hey, Jon." Came Alex's voice. "Are, are you at your dorm?"

"Yeah." He replied. "But, it's curfew now. Visiting hours are done."

"I see." Alex said. "And… How are you so far?" There was an odd sadness in Alex's tone; something that Jonathan was quick to notice. Why did Alex sound sad? Perhaps…he was feeling regretful?

"Same old, same old. Listen…about earlier…" Jonathan sighed and replied. "I'm sorry I punched you in the face."

"I probably deserved that." Alex said. "And….and I'm sorry I lied to you about…about your admission."

"Yeah. I mean, you were only looking out for me, right?" Jonathan asked. "You weren't just doing it for self-gratification or any of that?"

"No…" Alex replied, the same melancholic tone still evident in his voice. "You know I'm always looking out for you, right?"

"You have a pretty weird way of doing it." Jonathan chuckled.

"Well, at least you forgive me about what I did, right?" Alex asked

"I can't stay mad all the time. You're my brother." Jonathan said.

"Thank you, Jon." Alex said. "Hey, umm...tomorrow's the big day. Will you be there?"

"Alex...I..." Jonathan hesitated for a moment. He didn't really like attending ceremonies and events that had lots of people. But, on the other hand, he did tell Artemis he was going to support his brother. "Yeah, me and Artemis will be there."

"Great." Alex replied "Having you there...is the only thing that matters to me. Having you there witness the legacy I'm being honored for...is more important to me."

'Legacy being honored for.' Immediately, the words Alex uttered made Jonathan suddenly remember the nightmare he had. The nightmare about Alex and the Lady. The nightmare where Alex wanted to leave a legacy like no other...

"Alex, there's something I want to ask you." He said. But just before Jonathan could continue, Alex dropped the call. Jonathan tried to call him back, but all he got was a busy tone. 'Maybe a business call.' He thought. At the same time, he couldn't help but worry. Alex sounded quite sad when he spoke to him. Did he really feel that bad? Or was it something else?

'I could ask him tomorrow.' He said to himself. Just the two of us. After the ceremony.

****

Fridays at Berkeley were usually the least hectic of the school days, as they generally had no class schedules, and most students would use this day to either work on their school clubs, or unwind off campus. But on this particular Friday, the university was brimming with life. There was an excited commotion in the air, and it seemed to be coming from the new building.

There were tents propped up that housed several tall cocktail tables covered with white cloth. On top of the tables were small centerpieces and small platters of finger foods. Near the cocktail tables, a long table stood with rows of covered dishes on top. There were chairs arranged facing the front of the building. And in front of the rows of chairs, were two floral pillars that held a red ribbon tied in a bow. There were waiters who were walking around, serving several people who stood by the cocktail tables, eating a bit of the finger foods and sipping small glasses filled with drinks.

Jonathan marveled at the sight of the setup. He had to admit, the university really went all out. "Wow, all this for a ribbon cutting ceremony?" Artemis asked as she and Jonathan walked over to a cocktail table and ate a little of the peanuts served.

A waiter approached them and offered them drinks. Jonathan took a small glass of punch and drank it in one gulp. "Where is Alex?" He asked. "I didn't see him at all this morning and he won't answer my phone calls."

"Maybe he's with the university president." She suggested. "Or he's on his way?"

"Maybe." He agreed. "I...I spoke to him last night."

"And?" She asked.

"We talked." He replied. "And he suddenly apologized for the whole admissions and stuff."

"That's good right?" She said. "See, deep down your brother really cares about you. All you had to do was talk."

"Yeah, but he sounded very sad." He added.

"Maybe he really felt awful about it, and you punching him must have made him really think about it." She suggested as she ate some more peanuts. 'Maybe,' he thought to himself. But he was still bothered by the fact that Alex sounded almost sad on the phone. He wondered why…

Just then, they heard a man speaking on the microphone, asking everyone to take their seats. As they sat down, the university president walked up to the front and welcomed everyone. "Welcome, dear guests. Today is a very special day." He began. "I thank you for taking the time out of your busy schedules to be a part of this historic event in our university's history."

"Some of you have attended this university before, and right after graduation, made names for yourselves in your respective industry." He continued. "But today, we honor one particular individual who has made a name for himself during and after his school years. I personally met this young individual when he took home the championship trophy during the now famous 'Miracle from the Heavens' game."

'And here we go.' Jonathan muttered as they listened to the university president's speech. Finally, after what seemed like hours of speaking, the university president then said. "Please help me welcome the pride of our university and the namesake of our new building. Alexander 'Alex' Madden!"

There was a roar of cheers and applause, as Alex Madden walked up to the center and stood next to the university president. Of course, there had to be a grand entrance. Jonathan muttered under his breath. After shaking hands with the president and board members, Alex stood in front of the crowd and spoke.

"Thank you very much for joining me. It feels so good to be back home in Berkeley and to give it the much-needed pride it deserves." The crowd clapped and cheered and Jonathan, not wanting to spoil the mood of sorts, clapped as well. He had to admit; Alex knew how to command an audience.

"This is a very special day in my life and I am very pleased to share it with all of you." He continued. "I hope this hall and its future residents will carry on the legacy of hard work and ingenuity that I have strived very hard to foster and cultivate."

The university president then produced two large scissors and handed one pair to Alex. They walked towards the floral podiums and each held the ribbon in their hands. With the scissors, Alex and the university president cut the ribbon. The crowd clapped and cheered as they were ushered inside the newly opened Alexander Madden Hall.

Jonathan and Artemis followed the crowd inside, marveling at the sheer elegance of the Hall. Jonathan then decided to go and speak to Alex. He craned his head up to see where his brother was. He saw his brother speaking to several other guests. He then told Artemis where he was headed and began to make his way towards Alex, when he was suddenly approached by a group of people who began to ask him questions.

"Hey, you're Alex's brother, right?" a woman asked.

"I bet you're mighty proud of your brother." A man said.

"You must be wondering how you're going to follow your big bro's steps, huh?" said another man.

'I don't have time for this.' Jonathan thought as he excused himself and weaved his way across the floor towards where Alex was. He reached the space and saw that Alex was gone. 'Where did Alex go?' He looked around once more and then...he froze on where he stood. He gasped at what he was seeing.

Not too far from where he stood, he saw a woman covered in layers of silk and a silk cloth covered half of her face. The Lady! He said under his breath as he stared at her. He watched as the Lady looked at him with a stony gaze before walking away. Jonathan quickly followed the Lady and saw her standing at the end of a hallway.

"What are you doing here?" He called out to her. "Who summoned you?!" The Lady looked at him and he could feel the icy, stony gaze from her visible eyes.

One could only imagine what he was feeling when he spoke to her. Adrenaline rushing inside his being; the very notion of addressing a spectral being, that by today's standards, would be deemed impossible; one could even say that Jonathan was communicating with something that should never be taken lightly.

The Lady was silent, prompting Jonathan to ask yet again. "Who are you taking this time?"

The Lady lifted a finger and pointed upwards. Jonathan looked to the direction and then back at the Lady. She had disappeared. Suddenly, there came a panicked scream.

"ALEX MADDEN IS ON THE ROOF!"

At that moment, all the guests and visitors filed out of the hall and into the grounds. Jonathan followed the crowd and saw Artemis and the rest of the crowd looking up in complete horror and disbelief. Jonathan turned around to see, and true to the panicked cry, there on top of the new hall stood Alex Madden looking down with a look of despair on his face.

"ALEX!" Jonathan cried out. "WHAT THE HELL!?"

"I.... I must." He heard Alex speak. Quickly acting on logic and instinct, Jonathan ran back into the building and climbed up the many flight of stairs until he reached the rooftop. He slammed the door wide open and saw Alex standing closer to the edge.

Jonathan began to walk towards Alex and stated. "Alex, what are you even-?"

"STAY BACK!" Alex bellowed. "Stay back, Jonathan." He looked down at the ground below him. Jonathan hesitated for a moment before slowly moving forward, taking care not to make huge steps.

"Alex, get off the edge, please." He said. "Why are you even here?"

"I'm sorry, Jon." Alex replied as if completely ignoring Jonathan's question. "I am not what you think I am."

"What the hell are you talking about?" Jonathan asked. "Are you high or drunk? We can talk about this..." He was genuinely worried about Alex. This was not like him. It was like he was acting like a completely different person.

"I am a fraud, Jon." He heard Alex say. "A fraud and a fool. I should have known..." He started to fiddle with his finger.

'Known what?' Jonathan then saw him twisting a ring on his finger. He squinted for a bit and noticed it was the red ruby ring. He then remembered seeing the Lady earlier and how she pointed her finger up. 'No, it couldn't be.' He thought. 'There was no way...'

"I should have known Jon. I wasn't strong enough..." Alex said.

"Alex, what did you do?" Jonathan asked. "Did you.... did you summon the Lady on the Horse?"

"I wasn't strong enough, Jon." He replied. "I am not as strong as you are. I wanted to be the person everyone talked about. But I couldn't handle it alone. So... I..."

"What did you ask her?" Jonathan begged in his heart and mind for Alex to answer a different question, or at the very least not answer at all. He didn't want to believe the nightmare he had...was real.

"Do you remember when I gave you advice about how to survive college?" he asked. "Your eyes were full of excitement when I told you about Berkeley. You were still in the sixth grade, but you already knew what you wanted."

"Alex, why aren't you answering me?" Jonathan asked, his voice slowly breaking. "Please tell me what you did..."

"When you asked me about Berkeley, I was determined to inspire you." He replied as he slowly began to move even closer to the edge of the building. Jonathan could hear gasps and pleas from the crowd below, begging Alex to step away from the edge.

"Alex, please step away from the edge." He begged. "Whatever you're feeling we can talk it over..."

"I betrayed your trust." Alex looked at Jonathan. "I lied because I was too proud to admit it. But you were stronger than me. You couldn't care less what others said about you or your decisions. But I wanted to protect you. Inspire you..."

"Just get away from the edge and we can talk about it." Jonathan said. "Look I'm not mad at you. Just talk to me. Please." For the first time in a long time, Jonathan felt like the little boy who idolized his older brother, and who would run to him whenever he would cry and feel awful. "Please, Alex." He begged once more. "Let me help you..."

"I asked her to grant my wish." Alex said, looking down at the ground below. "I wished to leave a legacy unlike any other. And I got it."

'No,' Jonathan thought. 'It couldn't be.' He then said. "Alex, step away from the edge and we'll try to find a way to help you."

"Do you forgive me, Jon?" Alex said. "For lying to you? For disappointing you?"

"Look, I forgive you! You're my brother. Now please get down and let me help you." He pleaded.

Alex looked over his shoulder and in a weak and strained voice, said. "Be strong, Jon." Then he put his foot forward and in what felt like time moving slow, Jonathan watched in horror as Alex, his only brother, stepped off the edge of the roof and plummeted five floors to the ground below. There came a loud thud, followed by screams of horror and anguish.

Jonathan ran to the edge of the building and looked at the bottom. Sprawled below in a pool of his own blood, was the lifeless body of Alex Madden. In that one moment, Jonathan felt as though someone had ripped his heart out. He gripped unto the edge of the roof and began to let out deep, labored breaths.

'This wasn't happening.' He muttered to himself, fighting back several tears from falling down his face. 'Alex...' He looked down once more and saw a mist forming behind the crowd. He could see the same horrific sight he saw on the night of Claire's death. The veiled Lady astride a white horse. And standing next to the Lady was the faint figure of his older brother, Alex.

He watched as the Lady guided her horse towards the mist and both she and Alex disappeared into the foggy mist. Jonathan looked on in utter disbelief, and let out an anguished and pained cry that echoed throughout the entire campus.